Reese Ryan writes sexy, deeply emotional romances full of family drama, surprising secrets and unexpected twists.

Born and raised in the Midwest, Reese has deep Tennessee roots. Every summer, she endured long, hot car trips to family reunions in Memphis via a tiny clown car loaded with cousins.

Connect with Reese at ReeseRyanWrites on Instagram, Twitter and Facebook or at reeseryan.com/desirereaders.

His Until Midnight

REESE RYAN

MILLS & BOON

First published in Great Britain 2018
by Mills & Boon, an imprint of HarperCollins*Publishers*
1 London Bridge Street, London, SE1 9GF

Large Print edition 2019

© 2018 Harlequin Books S.A.

Special thanks and acknowledgement are given to
Reese Ryan for her contribution to the
Texas Cattleman's Club: Bachelor Auction miniseries.

ISBN: 978-0-263-08330-9

MIX
Paper from
responsible sources
FSC™ C007454

This book is produced from independently certified FSC™ paper to ensure responsible forest management. For more information visit www.harpercollins.co.uk/green.

Printed and bound in Great Britain
by CPI Group (UK) Ltd, Croydon, CR0 4YY

To Johnathan Royal,
Stephanie Perkins, Jennifer Copeland,
Denise Stokes, Sharon Blount,
Stephanie Douglas-Quick and all of the
amazing readers in the Reese Ryan VIP
Readers Lounge on Facebook. Seriously,
y'all rock! I appreciate your readership,
engagement, enthusiasm and
continued support. Thank you to
each and every one of you!

To my infinitely patient and ever-
insightful editor, Charles Griemsman,
thank you for all you do.

One

Tessa Noble stared at the configuration of high and low balls scattered on the billiard table.

"I'm completely screwed," she muttered, sizing up her next move. After a particularly bad break and distracted play, she was losing badly.

But how on earth could she be expected to concentrate on billiards when her best friend Ryan Bateman was wearing a fitted performance T-shirt that highlighted every single pectoral muscle and his impressive biceps. He could have, at the very least, worn a shirt that fit, instead of one that was a size too small, as a way to purposely enhance his muscles. And the view when he bent over the table in a pair of broken-in jeans that hugged his firm ass like they were made for it…

How in the hell was she expected to play her best?

"You're not screwed," Ryan said in a deep, husky voice that was as soothing as a warm bath. Three parts sex-in-a-glass and one part confidence out the wazoo.

Tessa's cheeks heated, inexplicably. Like she was a middle schooler giggling over double entendres and sexual innuendo.

"Maybe not, but you'd sure as hell like to be screwed by your best friend over there," Gail Walker whispered in her ear before taking another sip of her beer.

Tessa elbowed her friend in the ribs, and the woman giggled, nearly shooting beer out of her nose.

Gail, always a little too direct, lacked a filter after a second drink.

Tessa walked around the billiard table, pool cue in hand, assessing her options again while her opponent huffed restlessly. Finally, she shook her head and sighed. "You obviously see something I don't, because I don't see a single makeable shot."

Ryan sidled closer, his movements reminiscent of a powerful jungle cat stalking prey. His green eyes gleamed even in the dim light of the bar.

"You're underestimating yourself, Tess," Ryan murmured. "Just shut out all the noise, all the doubts, and focus."

She studied the table again, tugging her lower lip between her teeth, before turning back to him. "Ryan, I clearly don't have a shot."

"Go for the four ball." He nodded toward the purple ball wedged between two of her opponent's balls.

Tessa sucked in a deep breath and gripped the pool cue with one hand. She pressed her other hand to the table, formed a bridge and positioned the stick between her thumb and forefinger, gliding it back and forth.

But the shot just wasn't there.

"I can't make this shot." She turned to look at him. "Maybe you could, but I can't."

"That's because you're too tight, and your stance is all wrong." Ryan studied her for a moment, then placed his hands on either side of her waist and shifted her a few inches. "Now you're lined up with the ball. That should give you a better sight line."

Tessa's eyes drifted closed momentarily as she tried to focus on the four ball, rather than the lingering heat from Ryan's hands. Or his nearness as he hovered over her.

She opened them again and slid the cue back and forth between her fingers, deliberating the position and pace of her shot.

"Wait." Ryan leaned over beside her. He slipped an arm around her waist and gripped the stick a few inches above where she clenched it. He stared straight ahead at the ball, his face inches from hers. "Loosen your grip on the cue. This is a finesse shot, so don't try to muscle it. Just take it easy and smack the cue ball right in the center, and you've got this. Okay?"

"Okay." Tessa nodded, staring at the center of the white ball. She released a long breath, pulled back the cue and hit the cue ball dead in the center, nice and easy.

The cue ball connected with the four ball with a smack. The purple ball rolled toward the corner pocket and slowed, teetering on the edge. But it had just enough momentum to carry it over into the pocket.

"Yes!" Tessa squealed, smacking Ryan's raised palm to give him a high five. "You're amazing. You actually talked me through it."

"You did all the work. I was just your cheering section." He winked in that way that made her tummy flutter.

"Well, thank you." She smiled. "I appreciate it."

"What are best friends for?" He shrugged, picking up his beer and taking a sip from the bottle.

"Thought I was playing Tess," Roy Jensen grumbled. "Nobody said anything about y'all tag-teaming me."

"Oh, quit complaining, you old coot." Tessa stared down her opponent. "I always turn a blind eye when you ask for spelling help when we're playing Scrabble."

Roy's cheeks tinged pink, and he mumbled under his breath as Tessa moved around the table, deciding which shot to take next. She moved toward the blue two ball.

"Hey, Ryan." Lana, the way-too-friendly barmaid, sidled up next to him, her chest thrust forward and a smile as wide as the Rio Grande spread across her face. "Thought you might want another beer."

"Why thank you, kindly." Ryan tipped an imaginary hat and returned the grin as he accepted the bottle.

Tessa clenched her jaw, a burning sensation in her chest. She turned to her friend, whispering so neither Lana nor Ryan could hear her.

"Why doesn't she just take his head and smash it between the surgically enhanced boobs her ex-boyfriend gave her as a consolation prize? It'd be a lot easier for both of them."

"Watch it there, girl. You're beginning to sound

an awful lot like a jealous girlfriend." Gail could barely contain her grin.

"There's nothing to be jealous of. Ryan and I are just friends. You know that."

"*Best* friends," her friend pointed out, as she studied Ryan flirting with Lana. "But let's face it. You're two insanely attractive people. Are you really going to try and convince me that neither of you has ever considered—"

"We haven't." Tessa took her shot, missing badly. It was a shot she should've hit, even without Ryan's help. But she was too busy eavesdropping on his conversation with Lana.

"Well, for a person who doesn't have any romantic interest in her best friend, you seem particularly interested in whether or not he's flirting with the big-boobed barmaid." Gail shrugged when Tessa gave her the stink eye. "What? You know it's true."

Tessa scowled at her friend's words and the fact that Roy was taking advantage of her distraction. He easily sank one ball, then another. With no more striped balls left on the table, Roy had a clear shot at the eight ball.

He should be able to make that shot blindfolded.

"Well?" Gail prodded her.

"I'm not jealous of Lana. I just think Ryan could do better. That he *should* do better than to fall for the calculated ploy of a woman who has dollar signs in her eyes. Probably angling for butt implants this time."

Gail giggled. "And why would he want a fake ass when he was mere inches from the real deal?" She nodded toward Tessa's behind, a smirk on her face.

Tessa was fully aware that she'd inherited her generous curves from her mother. She was just as clear about Ryan Bateman's obliviousness to them. To him, she was simply one of the guys. But then again, the comfy jeans and plaid button-down shirts that filled her closet didn't do much to highlight her assets.

Hadn't that been the reason she'd chosen such a utilitarian wardrobe in the first place?

"Dammit!" Roy banged his pool cue on the

wooden floor, drawing their attention to him. He'd scratched on the eight ball.

Tessa grinned. "I won."

"Because I scratched." Roy's tone made it clear that he felt winning by default was nothing to be proud of.

"A win's a win, Jensen." She wriggled her fingers, her palm open. "Pay up."

"You won? Way to go, Tess. I told you that you had this game in the bag." Ryan, suddenly beside her, wrapped a big, muscular arm around her shoulder and pulled her into a half hug.

"Well, at least one of us believed in me." Tessa counted the four wrinkled five-dollar bills Roy stuffed in her palm begrudgingly.

"Always have, always will." He beamed at her and took another swig of his beer.

Tessa tried to ignore the warmth in her chest that filtered down her spine and fanned into areas she didn't want to acknowledge.

Because they were friends. And friends didn't get all...whatever it was she was feeling...over one another. Not even when they looked and smelled good enough to eat.

Tessa Noble always smelled like citrus and sunshine. Reminded him of warm summer picnics at the lake. Ryan couldn't peel an orange or slice a lemon without thinking of her and smiling.

There was no reason for his arm to still be wrapped around her shoulder other than the sense of comfort he derived from being this close to her.

"Take your hands off my sister, Bateman." Tessa's brother Tripp's expression was stony as he entered the bar. As if he was about five minutes away from kicking Ryan's ass.

"Tessa just beat your man, Roy, here." Ryan didn't move. Nor did he acknowledge Tripp's veiled threat.

The three of them had been friends forever, though it was Tessa who was his best friend. According to their parents, their friendship was born the moment they first met. Their bond had only gotten stronger over the years. Still, he'd had to assure Tripp on more than one occasion that his relationship with Tess was purely platonic.

Relationships weren't his gift. He'd made peace with that, particularly since the dissolution of his engagement to Sabrina Calhoun little more than a year ago. Tripp had made it clear, in a joking-not-joking manner, that despite their longtime friendship, he'd punch his lights out if Ryan ever hurt his sister.

He couldn't blame the guy. Tess definitely deserved better.

"Way to go, Tess." A wide grin spread across Tripp's face. He gave his sister a fist bump, followed by a simulated explosion.

The Nobles' signature celebratory handshake.

"Thanks, Tripp." Tessa casually stepped away from him.

Ryan drank his beer, captivated by her delectable scent which still lingered in the air around him.

"You look particularly proud of yourself today, big brother." Tessa raised an eyebrow, her arms folded.

The move inadvertently framed and lifted Tessa's rather impressive breasts. Another feature he tried hard, as her best friend, to not notice. But then again, he was a guy, with guy parts and a guy brain.

Ryan quickly shifted his gaze to Tripp's. "You still pumped about being a bachelor in the Texas Cattleman's Club charity auction?"

Tripp grinned like a prize hog in the county fair, his light brown eyes—identical to his sister's—twinkling merrily. "Alexis Slade says I'll fetch a mint."

"Hmm…" Ryan grinned. "Tess, what do you think your brother here will command on the auction block?"

"Oh, I'd say four maybe even five…dollars." Tessa, Ryan, Gail and Roy laughed hysterically, much to Tripp's chagrin.

Tripp folded his arms over his chest. "I see you all have jokes tonight."

"You know we're just kidding." Ryan, who had called next, picked up a pool cue as Roy gathered the balls and racked them. "After all, I'm the one who suggested you to Alexis."

"And I may never forgive you for creating this monster." Tessa scowled at Ryan playfully.

"My bad, I wasn't thinking." He chuckled.

"What I want to know is why on earth you didn't volunteer yourself?" Gail asked. "You're a moderately good-looking guy, if you like that sort of thing." She laughed.

She was teasing him, not flirting. Though with Gail it was often hard to tell.

Ryan shrugged. "I'm not interested in parading across the stage for a bunch of desperate women to bid on, like I'm a side of beef." He glanced apologetically at his friend, Tripp. "No offense, man."

"None taken." Tripp grinned proudly, poking a thumb into his chest. "This 'side of beef' is chomping at the bit to be taken for a spin by one of the lovely ladies."

Tessa elbowed Ryan in the gut, and an involuntary "oomph" sound escaped. "Watch it, Bateman. We aren't *desperate*. We're civic-minded women whose only interest is the betterment of our community."

There was silence for a beat before Tessa and Gail dissolved into laughter.

Tessa was utterly adorable, giggling like a schoolgirl. The sound—rooted in his earliest memories of her—instantly conjured a smile that began deep down in his gut.

He studied her briefly. Her curly, dark brown hair was pulled into a low ponytail and her smooth, golden brown skin practically glowed. She was wearing her typical winter attire: a long-sleeved plaid shirt, jeans which hid her curvy frame rather than highlighting it, and the newest addition to her ever-growing sneaker collection.

"You're a brave man." Ryan shifted his attention to Tripp as he leaned down and lined his stick up with the cue ball. He drew it back and forth between his forefinger and thumb. "If these two are any indication—" he nodded toward Tess and Gail "—those women at the auction are gonna eat you alive."

"One can only hope." Tripp wriggled his brows

and held up his beer, one corner of his mouth curled in a smirk.

Ryan shook his head, then struck the white cue ball hard. He relished the loud cracking sound that indicated a solid break. The cue ball smashed through the triangular formation of colorful balls, and they rolled or spun across the table. A high and a low ball dropped into the pockets.

"Your choice." Ryan nodded toward Tessa.

"Low." Hardly a surprise. Tessa always chose low balls whenever she had first choice. She walked around the table, her sneakers squeaking against the floor, as she sized up her first shot.

"You know I'm only teasing you, Tripp. I think it's pretty brave of you to put yourself out there like that. I'd be mortified by the thought of anyone bidding on me." She leaned over the table, her sights on the blue two ball before glancing up at her brother momentarily. "In fact, I'm proud of you. The money you'll help raise for the Pancreatic Cancer Research Foundation will do a world of good."

She made her shot and sank the ball before lining up for the next one.

"Would you bid on a bachelor?" Ryan leaned against his stick, awaiting his turn.

He realized that Tess was attending the bachelor auction, but the possibility that she'd be bidding on one of them hadn't occurred to him until just now. And the prospect of his best friend going on a date with some guy whose company she'd paid for didn't sit well with him.

The protective instinct that had his hackles up was perfectly natural. He, Tripp and Tessa had had each others' backs since they were kids. They weren't just friends, they were family. Though Tess was less like a little sister and more like a really hot distant cousin, three times removed.

"Of course, I'm bidding on a bachelor." She sank another ball, then paced around the table and shrugged. "That's kind of the point of the entire evening."

"Doesn't mean you have to. After all, not every woman attending will be bidding on a bachelor," Ryan reminded her.

"They will be if they aren't married or engaged," Gail said resolutely, folding her arms and cocking an eyebrow his way. "Why, Ryan Bateman, sounds to me like you're jealous."

"Don't be ridiculous." His cheeks heated as he returned his gaze to the table. "I'm just looking out for my best friend. She shouldn't be pressured to participate in something that makes her feel uncomfortable."

Tessa was sweet, smart, funny, and a hell of a lot of fun to hang out with. But she wasn't the kind of woman he envisioned with a paddle in her hand, bidding on men as if she were purchasing steers at auction.

"Doesn't sound like Tess, to me. That's all I'm saying." He realized he sounded defensive.

"*Good.* It's about time I do something unexpected. I'm too predictable...too boring." Tessa cursed under her breath when she missed her shot.

"Also known as consistent and reliable," Ryan interjected.

Things were good the way they were. He liked

that Tessa followed a routine he could count on. His best friend's need for order balanced out his spontaneity.

"I know, but lately I've been feeling… I don't know…stifled. Like I need to take some risks in my personal life. Stop playing it so safe all the time." She sighed in response to his wide-eyed, slack-jawed stare. "Relax, Rye. It's not like I'm paying for a male escort."

"I believe they prefer the term *gigolo*," Gail, always helpful, interjected, then took another sip of her drink.

Ryan narrowed his gaze at Gail, which only made the woman laugh hysterically. He shifted his attention back to Tessa, who'd just missed her shot.

"Who will you be bidding on?"

Tessa shrugged. "I don't know. No one in particular in mind, just yet. The programs go out in a few days. Maybe I'll decide then. Or… I don't know…maybe I'll wait and see who tickles my fancy when I get there."

"Who *tickles your fancy*?" Ryan repeated the

words incredulously. His grip on the pool cue tightened.

He didn't like the sound of that at all.

Two

Tessa followed the sound of moaning down the hall and around the corner to her brother's room.

"Tripp? Are you all right?" She tapped lightly on his partially opened bedroom door.

"No!" The word was punctuated by another moan, followed by, "I feel like I'm dying."

Tessa hurried inside his room, her senses quickly assailed by a pungent scent which she followed to his bathroom. He was hugging the porcelain throne and looking a little green.

"Did you go out drinking last night?"

"No. I think it's the tuna sandwich I got from

the gas station late last night on my way back in from Dallas."

"How many times have I told you? Gas station food after midnight? No *bueno*." She stood with her hands on her hips, looking down at her brother who looked like he might erupt again at any minute.

Austin Charles Noble III loved food almost as much as he loved his family. And usually he had a stomach like a tank. Impervious to just about anything. So whatever he'd eaten had to have been pretty bad.

"I'm taking you to Urgent Care."

"No, I just want to go to bed. If I can sleep it off for a few hours, I'm sure I'll be fine." He forced a smile, then immediately clutched his belly and cringed. "I'll be good as new for the bachelor auction."

"Shit. The bachelor auction." Tess repeated the words. It was the next night. And as green at the gills as Tripp looked, there was little chance he'd be ready to be paraded on stage in front of a crowd of eager women by then. The way he looked now, he probably wouldn't fetch more than five dollars and a bottle of ipecac at auction.

"Here, let me help you back to bed." She leaned down, allowing her brother to drape his arm around her and get enough leverage to climb to his feet on unsteady legs. Once he was safely in bed again, she gathered the remains of the tainted tuna sandwich, an empty bottle of beer, and a few other items.

She set an empty garbage can with a squirt of soap and about an inch of water beside his bed.

"Use this, if you need to." She indicated the garbage can. "I'm going to get you some ginger ale and some Gatorade. But if you get worse, I'm taking you to the doctor. Mom and Dad wouldn't be too happy with me if I let their baby boy die of food poisoning while they were away on vacation."

"Well, I am Mom's favorite, so…" He offered a weak smile as he invoked the argument they often teased each other about. "And don't worry about the auction, I'll be fine. I'm a warrior, sis. Nothing is going to come between me and—"

Suddenly he bolted out of bed, ran to the bathroom and slammed the door behind him.

Tessa shook her head. "You're staying right here in bed today and tomorrow, 'warrior.' I'll get Roy and the guys to take care of the projects that were on your list today. And I'll find a replacement for you in the auction. Alexis will understand."

Tripp mumbled his thanks through the bathroom door, and she set off to take care of everything she had promised him.

Tessa had been nursing her brother back to health and handling her duties at the ranch, as well as some of his. And she'd been trying all day to get in touch with Ryan.

Despite his reluctance to get involved in the auction, he was the most logical choice as Tripp's replacement. She was sure she could convince him it was a worthy cause. Maybe stroke his ego and tell him there would be a feeding frenzy for a hot stud like him.

A statement she planned to make in jest, but

that she feared also had a bit of truth to it. Tessa gritted her teeth imagining Lana, and a whole host of other women in town who often flirted with Ryan, bidding on him like he was a prize steer.

Maybe getting Ryan to step in as Tripp's replacement in the auction wasn't such a good idea after all. She paced the floor, scrolling through a list of names of other possible options in her head.

Most of the eligible men that came to mind were already participating, or they'd already turned Alexis and Rachel down, from what Tessa had heard.

She stopped abruptly mid-stride, an idea brewing in her head that made her both excited and feel like she was going to toss her lunch at the same time.

"Do something that scares you every single day." She repeated the words under her breath that she'd recently posted on the wall of her office. It was a quote from Eleanor Roosevelt. Advice she'd promised herself that she would take to heart from here on out.

Tessa glanced at herself in the mirror. Her thick hair was divided into two plaits, and a Stetson was pushed down on her head, her eyes barely visible. She was the textbook definition of Plain Jane. Not because she wasn't attractive, but because she put zero effort into looking like a desirable woman rather than one of the ranch hands.

She sighed, her fingers trembling slightly. There was a good chance that Alexis and Rachel would veto her idea for Tripp's replacement. But at least she would ask.

Tessa pulled her cell phone out of her back pocket and scrolled through her contacts for Alexis Slade's number. Her palms were damp as she initiated the call. Pressing the phone to her ear, she counted the rings, a small part of her hoping that Alexis didn't answer. That would give her time to rethink her rash decision. Maybe save herself some embarrassment when Alexis rejected the idea.

"Hey, Tess. How are you?" Alexis's warm, cheerful voice rang through the line.

"I'm good. Tripp? Not so much. I think he has food poisoning." The words stumbled out of her mouth.

"Oh my God! That's terrible. Poor Tripp. Is he going to be okay?"

"I'm keeping an eye on him, but I'm sure he'll be fine in a few days. I just don't think he's going to recover in time to do the bachelor auction."

"We'll miss having him in the lineup, but of course we understand. His health is the most important thing." The concern was evident in Alexis's voice. "Tell him that we hope he's feeling better soon. And if the auction goes well, maybe we'll do this again next year. I'll save a spot in the lineup for him then."

"Do you have anyone in mind for a replacement?" Tessa paced the floor.

"Not really. We've pretty much tapped out our list of possibilities. Unless you can get Ryan to change his mind?" She sounded hopeful.

"I considered that, and I've been trying to reach

him all day. But just now, I came up with another idea." She paused, hoping that Alexis would stop her. Tell her that they didn't need anyone else. When the woman didn't respond, she continued. "I was thinking that I might replace my brother in the lineup." She rushed the words out before she could chicken out. "I know that this is a bachelor auction, not a bachelorette—"

"Yes!" Alexis squealed, as if it were the best idea she'd heard all day. "OMG, I think that's an absolutely fabulous idea. We'll provide something for the fellas, too. Oh, Tessa, this is brilliant. I love it."

"Are you sure? I mean, I like the idea of doing something completely unexpected, but maybe we should see what Rachel thinks." Her heart hammered in her chest.

She'd done something bold, something different, by offering to take Tripp's place. But now, the thought of actually walking that stage and praying to God that someone…anyone…would bid on her was giving her heart palpitations.

"That's a good idea, but I know she's going to agree with me. Hold on."

"Oh, you're calling her now?" Tessa said to the empty room as she paced the floor.

Rachel Kincaid was a marketing genius and an old college friend of Alexis's. She'd come to Royal as a young widow and the mother to an adorable little girl named Ellie. And she'd fallen in love with one of the most eligible bachelors in all of Texas, oil tycoon Matt Galloway.

"Okay, Rachel's on the line," Alexis announced a moment later. "And I brought her up to speed."

"You weren't kidding about doing something unexpected." There was a hint of awe in Rachel's voice. "Good for you, Tess."

"Thanks, Rachel." She swallowed hard. "But do you think it's a good idea? I mean, the programs have already been printed, and no one knows that there's going to be a bachelorette in the auction. What if no one bids on me? I don't want to cause any embarrassment to the club or create negative publicity for the event."

"Honey, the bachelors who aren't in the auction are going to go crazy when they discover there's a beautiful lady to bid on," Rachel said confidently.

"We'll put the word out that there's going to be a big surprise, just for the fellas. I can email everyone on our mailing list. It will only take me a few minutes to put the email together and send it out," Alexis said.

"Y'all are sure we can pull this off?" Tess asked one last time. "I swear I won't be offended if you think we can't. I rather you tell me now than to let me get up there and make a fool of myself."

"It's going to be awesome," Alexis reassured her. "But I'm sensing hesitation. Are you second-guessing your decision? Because you shouldn't. It's a good one."

Tessa grabbed a spoon and the pint of her favorite Neapolitan ice cream hidden in the back of the freezer. She sat at the kitchen island and sighed, rubbing her palm on her jeans again. She shook her head, casting another glance in the mirror. "It's just that… I'm not the glamorous type, that's for sure."

"You're gorgeous, girl. And if you're concerned… hey, why don't we give you a whole beauty make-over for the event?" Rachel said excitedly. "It'll be fun and it gives me another excuse to buy makeup."

"That's a fantastic idea, Rachel!" Alexis chimed in. "Not that you need it," she added. "But maybe it'll make you feel more comfortable."

"Okay, yeah. That sounds great. I'd like that." Tessa nodded, feeling slightly better. "I was gonna take tomorrow off anyway. Give myself plenty of time to get ready. But I'm sure you both have a million things to do. I don't want to distract you from preparing for the auction, just to babysit me."

"Alexis is the queen of organization. She's got everything under control. Plus, we have a terrific crew of volunteers," Rachel piped in. "They won't miss us for a few hours. I promise, everything will be fine."

"Have you considered what date you're offering?"

"Date?" Tessa hadn't thought that far in advance. "I'm not sure. I guess…let me think about that. I'll have an answer for you by tomorrow. Is that all right?"

"That's fine. Just let me know first thing in the morning," Alexis said.

"I'll make a few appointments for the make-over and I'll text you both all the details." Rachel's voice brimmed with excitement.

"Then I guess that's everything," Tessa said, more to herself than her friends. "I'll see you both tomorrow."

She hung up the phone, took a deep breath, and shoveled a spoonful of Neapolitan ice cream into her mouth.

There was no turning back now.

Three

Ryan patted the warm neck of his horse, Phantom, and dismounted, handing the majestic animal off to Ned, one of his ranch hands. He gave the horse's haunches one final pat as the older man led him away to a stall.

Ryan wiped his sweaty forehead with the back of his hand. He was tired, dirty and in desperate need of a shower.

He'd been out on the ranch and the surrounding area since the crack of dawn, looking for several steer that had made their great escape through a break in the fence. While his men repaired the fence, he and another hand tracked down the cattle and drove them back to the ranch.

He'd been in such a hurry to get after the cattle, he'd left his phone at home. Hopefully, his parents hadn't called, worried that he wasn't answering because he'd burned down the whole damn place.

He grumbled to himself, "You nearly burn the barn down as a kid, and they never let you forget it."

Then again, his parents and Tess and Tripp's seemed to be enjoying themselves on their cruise. Their calls had become far less frequent.

Who knows? Maybe both couples would decide it was finally time to retire, give up ranch life, and pass the torch to the next generation. Something he, Tessa and Tripp had been advocating for the past few years. They were ready to take on the responsibility.

When he'd been engaged to Sabrina, his parents had planned to retire to their beach house in Galveston and leave management of the ranch to him. Despite the fact that they hadn't much liked his intended. Not because Sabrina was a bad person. But he and Sabrina were like fire and ice. The moments that were good could be really good. But the moments that weren't had resulted in tense arguments and angry sex.

His mother, in particular, hadn't been convinced Sabrina was the girl for him. She'd been right.

A few months before their wedding, Sabrina had called it off. She just couldn't see herself as a ranch wife. Nor was she willing to sacrifice her well-earned figure to start "popping out babies" to carry on the Bateman name.

He appreciated that she'd had the decency to tell him to his face, well in advance, rather than abandoning him at the altar as Shelby Arthur had done when she'd decided she couldn't marry Jared Goodman.

At least she'd spared him *that* humiliation.

Besides, there was a part of him that realized the truth of what she'd said. Maybe some part of him had always understood that he'd asked her to marry him because it felt like the right thing to do.

He'd been with Sabrina longer than he'd stayed in any relationship. For over a year. So when she'd hinted that she didn't want to waste her time in a relationship that wasn't going anywhere, he'd popped the question.

Neither he nor Sabrina were the type who bought into the fairy tale of romance. They understood that relationships were an exchange. A series of transactions, sustained over time. Which was why he believed they were a good fit. But they'd both ignored an essential point. They were just too different.

He loved everything about ranch life, and Sabrina was a city girl, through and through.

The truth was that he'd been relieved when Sabrina had canceled the wedding. As if he could breathe, nice, deep, easy breaths, for the first time in months. Still, his parents called off their plans to retire.

Maybe this trip would convince them that he

and the Bateman Ranch would be just fine without them.

Ryan stretched and groaned. His muscles, taut from riding in the saddle a good portion of the day, protested as he made his way across the yard toward the house.

Helene Dennis, their longtime house manager, threw open the door and greeted him. "There you are. You look an unholy mess. Take off those boots and don't get my kitchen floor all dirty. I just mopped."

Sometimes he wondered if Helene worked for him or if he worked for her. Still, he loved the older woman. She was family.

"All right, all right." He toed off his boots and kicked them in the corner, patting his arms and legs to dislodge any dust from his clothing before entering the house. "Just don't shoot."

Helene playfully punched his arm. "Were you able to round up all of the animals that got loose?"

"Every one of them." Yawning, he kneaded a stubborn kink in his back. "Fence is fixed, too."

"Good. Dinner will be ready in about a half an hour. Go ahead and hop in the shower. Oh, and call Tess when you get the chance."

"Why?" His chest tightened. "Everything okay over at the Noble Spur?"

"Don't worry." She gave him a knowing smile that made his cheeks fill with heat. "She's fine, but her brother is ill. Tess is pretty sure it's food poisoning. She's been trying to reach you all day."

"I was in such a hurry to get out of here this morning, I forgot my phone."

"I know." She chuckled softly "I found it in the covers when I made your bed this morning. It's on your nightstand."

Managing a tired smile for the woman he loved almost as much as his own mother, he leaned in and kissed her cheek. "Thanks, Helene. I'll be down for dinner as soon as I can."

Ryan dried his hair from the shower and wrapped the towel around his waist. The hot water had felt good sluicing over his tired, aching muscles. So he'd taken a longer shower than he'd intended. And though he was hungry, he was tempted to collapse into bed and forgo dinner.

Sighing wearily, he sat on the bed and picked up his phone to call Tess.

She answered in a couple of rings. "Hey, Rye. How'd it go? Were you able to find all the steer you lost?"

Helene had evidently told her where he was and why he hadn't been answering his cell phone.

"Yes, we got them all back and the fence is fixed." He groaned as he reached out to pick up his watch and put it back on. "How's Tripp? Helene said he got food poisoning."

"Wow, you sound like you've been ridden hard and put away wet." She laughed. "And yes, my brother's penchant for late night snacks from suspect eateries finally caught up with him. He looks and feels like hell, but otherwise he's recovering."

"Will he be okay for the auction tomorrow?"

"No." She said the word a little too quickly, then paused a little too long. "He thinks he'll be fine to go through with it, but I'm chalking that up to illness-induced delusion."

"Did you tell Alexis she's a man down?"

"I did." There was another unusual pause. Like there was something she wanted to say but was hesitant.

Ryan thought for a moment as he rummaged through his drawers for something to put on.

"Ahh…" He dragged his fingers through his damp hair. "Of course. She wants to know if I'll take Tripp's place."

Tessa didn't respond right away. "Actually, that's why I was trying so hard to reach you. I thought I might be able to convince you to take Tripp's place…since it's for such a good cause. But when I couldn't reach you, I came up with another option."

"Which is?" It was like pulling teeth to get Tess to just spit it out. He couldn't imagine why that would be…unless he wasn't going to like what she had to say. Uneasiness tightened his gut. "So this other option…are you going to tell me, or should I come over and you can act it out in charades?"

"Smart-ass." She huffed. "No charades necessary. *I'm* the other option. I decided to take Tripp's place in the auction."

"You do know that it's women who will be bidding in this auction, right?" Ryan switched to speakerphone, tossed his phone on the bed, then stepped into his briefs. "Anything you need to tell me, Tess?"

"I'm going to give you a pass because I know you're tired," she groused. "And we've already considered that. If you check your in-box, you'll see that Alexis sent out an email informing all attendees and everyone else on the mailing list that there is going to be a surprise at the end of the auction, just for the gents."

"Oh."

It was the only thing that Ryan could think to say as the realization struck him in the gut like a bull running at full speed. A few days ago, he'd been discomfited by the idea of his friend bidding on one man. Now, there would be who knows how many guys angling for a night with her.

"You sure about this?" He stepped into a pair of

well-worn jeans and zipped and buttoned them.
"This just doesn't seem much like you."

"That's exactly why I'm doing it." Her voice
was shaky. "It'll be good for me to venture outside of my comfort zone."

He donned a long-sleeved T-shirt, neither of
them speaking for a moment.

Ryan rubbed his chin and sank on to his mattress. He slipped on a pair of socks. "Look, I
know I said I didn't want to do it, but with Tripp
being sick and all, how about I make an exception?"

"You think this is a really bad idea, don't you?"
She choked out the words, her feelings obviously
hurt.

"No, that's not what I'm saying at all." The last
thing he wanted to do was upset his best friend.
He ran a hand through his hair. "I'm just saying
that it's really last minute. And because of that,
it might take people by surprise, that's all."

"I thought of that, too. Alexis and Rachel are
positive they can drum up enough interest. But

I thought that…just to be safe…it'd be good to have an ace up my sleeve."

"What kind of an ace?"

"I'm going to give you the money to bid on me, in case no one else does. I know it'll still look pretty pathetic if my best friend is the only person who bids on me, but that's a hell of a lot better than hearing crickets when they call my name."

"You want me to bid on you?" He repeated the words. Not that he hadn't heard or understood her the first time. He was just processing the idea. Him bidding on his best friend. The two of them going out on a date…

"Yes, but it'll be my money. And there's no need for us to actually go on the date. I mean, we can just hang out like usual or something, but it doesn't have to be a big deal."

"Sure, I'll do it. But you don't need to put up the money. I'm happy to make the donation myself."

His leg bounced. Despite what his friend believed, Ryan doubted that he'd be the only man there willing to bid on Tessa Noble during her bachelorette auction.

"Thanks, Ryan. I appreciate this." She sounded relieved. "And remember, you'll only need to bid on me if no one else does. If nothing else, your bid might prompt someone else to get into the spirit."

"Got it," he said gruffly. "You can count on me."

"I know. Thanks again, Rye." He could hear the smile in her sweet voice.

"Hey, since Tripp won't be able to make it… why don't we ride in together?"

"Actually, I'm going straight to the auction from…somewhere else. But I'll catch a ride with a friend, so we can ride home together. How's that?"

"Sounds good." He couldn't help the twinge of disappointment he felt at only getting to ride home with her. "I guess I'll see you there."

"I'll be the one with the price tag on her head." Tessa forced a laugh. "Get some rest, Rye. And take some pain meds. Otherwise, your arm'll be too sore to lift the auction paddle."

Her soft laughter was the last thing he heard before the line went dead. Before he could say good-night.

Ryan released a long sigh and slid his feet into his slippers. He didn't like the idea of Tess putting herself on the auction block for every letch in town to leer at. But she was a grown woman who was capable of making her own decisions.

Regardless of how much he disagreed with them.

Besides, he wasn't quite sure what it was that made him feel more uneasy. Tess being bid on by other men, or the idea that he might be the man who won her at the end of the night.

Four

Tessa had never been plucked, primped and prodded this much in her entire life.

She'd been waxed in places she didn't even want to think about and had some kind of wrap that promised to tighten her curves. And the thick head of curls she adored had been straightened and hung in tousled waves around her shoulders. Now Milan Valez, a professional makeup artist, was applying her makeup.

"I thought we were going with a natural look," Tess objected when the woman opened yet another product and started to apply what had to be a third or fourth layer of goop to her face.

"This *is* the natural look." The woman rolled her eyes. "If I had a dime for every client who doesn't realize that what they're calling the natural look is actually a full face." The woman sighed, but her expression softened as she directed Tess to turn her head. "You're a beautiful woman with gorgeous skin. If you're not a makeup wearer, I know it feels like a lot. But I'm just using a few tricks to enhance your natural beauty. We'll make those beautiful eyes pop, bring a little drama to these pouty lips, and highlight your incredible cheekbones. I promise you won't look too heavily made up. Just trust me."

Tessa released a quiet sigh and nodded. "I trust you."

"Good. Now just sit back and relax. Your friends should be here shortly. They're going to be very pleased, and I think you will, too." The woman smiled. "Now look up."

Tessa complied as Milan applied liner beneath her eyes. "You sure I can't have a little peek?"

"Your friends made me promise. No peeking. And you agreed." She lifted Tess's chin. "Don't worry, honey, you won't have to wait much longer."

"Tessa? Oh my God, you look…incredible." Rachel entered the salon a few minutes later and clapped a hand over her mouth. "I can hardly believe it's you."

Alexis nearly slammed into the back of Rachel, who'd made an abrupt stop. She started to complain, but when she saw Tessa, her mouth gaped open, too.

"Tess, you look…stunning. Not that you aren't always beautiful, but…wow. Just wow."

"You two are making me seriously self-conscious right now." Tessa kept her focus on Milan.

"Don't be," the woman said emphatically. "Remember what we talked about. I've only enhanced what was already there."

Tessa inhaled deeply and nodded. She ignored the butterflies in her stomach in response to the broad grins and looks of amazement on Alexis's and Rachel's faces.

"There, all done." Milan sat back proudly and grinned. "Honey, you look absolutely beautiful. Ready to see for yourself?"

"Please." Even as Tessa said it, her hands were trembling, and a knot tightened in her stomach. How could something as simple as looking in the mirror be so fraught with anxiety? It only proved she wasn't cut out for this whole glamour-girl thing.

Milan slowly turned the chair around and Alexis and Rachel came over to stand closer, both of them bouncing excitedly.

Tessa closed her eyes, took a deep breath and then opened them.

"Oh my God." She leaned closer to the mirror. "I can hardly believe that's me." She sifted her fingers through the dark, silky waves with toffee-colored highlights. "I mean, it looks like me, just…more glamourous."

"I know, isn't it incredible? You're going to be the star of the evening. We need to keep you hidden until you walk across the stage. Really take everyone by surprise." Rachel grinned in the mirror from behind her.

"Oh, that's a brilliant idea, Rachel," Alexis agreed. "It'll have more impact."

"This is only the beginning." Rachel's grin widened. "Just wait until they get a load of your outfit tonight. Every man in that room's jaw will hit the floor."

Tessa took another deep breath, then exhaled as she stared at herself in the mirror. Between her makeover and the daring outfit she'd chosen, there was no way Ryan, or anyone else, would take her for one of the boys.

Her heart raced and her belly fluttered as she anticipated his reaction. She couldn't wait to see the look of surprise on Ryan's face.

Ryan entered the beautiful gardens where The Great Royal Bachelor Auction was being held. Alexis Slade, James Harris and the rest of the committee had gone out of their way to create a festive and beautiful setting for the event. Fragrant wreaths and sprigs of greenery were strung from the pergolas. Two towering trees decorated with gorgeous ornaments dominated the area. Poinsettias, elegant red bows and white lights decorated the space, giving it a glowing, ethereal feel. The garden managed to be both romantic and festive. The kind of setting that almost made you regret not having someone to share the night with.

He sipped his Jack and Coke and glanced around the vicinity. Everyone who was anyone was in attendance. He made his way through the room, mingling with Carter Mackenzie and Shelby Arthur, Matt Galloway and Rachel Kincaid, Austin and Brooke Bradshaw, and all of the other members of the club who'd turned out for the event. Several of the bachelors moved around the space, drumming up anticipation for the auction and doing their best to encourage a bidding frenzy.

But Tessa was nowhere to be found. Had she changed her mind? He was looking forward to hanging out with her tonight, but he'd understand if she'd gotten cold feet. Hell, there was a part of him that was relieved to think that maybe she'd bailed.

Then again, Tess had said she'd be coming from somewhere else. So maybe she was just running late.

He resisted the urge to pull out his cell phone and find out exactly where she was. For once in his life, he'd be patient. Even if it killed him.

"Ryan, it's good to see you." James Harris, president of the Texas Cattleman's Club, shook his hand. "I hate that we couldn't convince you to be one of our bachelor's tonight, but I'm glad you joined us just the same."

"Didn't see your name on the list of bachelors either." Ryan smirked, and both men laughed.

"Touché." James took a gulp of his drink and Ryan did the same.

"Looks like y'all are doing just fine without me." Ryan gestured to the space. "I wouldn't have ever imagined this place could look this good."

"Alexis Slade outdid herself with this whole romantic winter wonderland vibe." James's eyes trailed around the space. "To be honest, I wasn't sure exactly how her vision would come together, but she's delivered in spades. I'm glad we gave her free rein to execute it as she saw fit."

"Judging from everyone here's reaction, you've got a hit on your hands." Ryan raised his glass before finishing the last of his drink.

"Let's just hope it motivates everyone to dig deep in their pockets tonight." James patted Ryan on the back. "I'd better go chat with Rose Clayton." He nodded toward the older woman, who looked stunning in her gown. The touch of gray hair at her temples gleamed in the light. "But I'll see you around."

"You bet." Ryan nodded toward the man as he traversed the space and greeted Rose.

"Ryan, how are you?" Gail Walker took a sip of her drink and grinned. "You look particularly handsome tonight. But I see Alexis still wasn't able to talk you into joining the list of eligible bachelors."

"Not my thing, but looks like they've got plenty of studs on the schedule for you to choose from."

Ryan sat his empty glass on a nearby tray. "And you clean up pretty well yourself."

"Thanks." She smoothed a hand over the skirt of her jewel-tone green dress. "But I've got my eye on one bachelor in particular." Her eyes shone with mischief. "And I'm prepared to do whatever it takes to get him."

"Well, I certainly wouldn't want to be the woman who has to run up against you." Ryan chuckled. "Good luck."

"Thanks, Ryan. See you around." Gail made her way through the crowd, mingling with other guests.

Ryan accepted a napkin and a few petite quiches from a server passing by. Ignoring the anticipation that made his heart beat a little faster as he considered the prospect of bidding on his friend.

Tessa paced the space that served as the bachelors' green room. Everyone else had spent most of the night mingling. They came to the green room once the start of the auction drew closer. But she'd been stuck here the entire evening, bid-ing her time until she was scheduled to make her grand entrance.

"Tessa Noble? God, you look…incredible." Daniel Clayton shoved a hand in his pocket. "But what are you doing here? Wait…are you the surprise?"

"Guilty." Her cheeks warmed as she bit into another quiche.

She tried her best not to ruin the makeup that Milan had so painstakingly applied. The woman had assured her that she could eat and drink without the lipstick fading or feathering. But Tess still found herself being extra careful.

"Everyone will definitely be surprised," he said, then added, "Not that you don't look good normally."

"It's okay, Daniel. I get it." She mumbled around a mouth full of quiche. "It was a surprise to me, too."

He chuckled, running a hand through his jet-black hair. "You must be tired of people telling you how different you look. How did Tripp and Ryan react?"

"Neither of them has seen me yet." She balled up her napkin and tossed it in the trash. "I'm a little nervous about their reaction."

"Don't be," Daniel said assuredly. "I can't imagine a man alive could find fault with the way you look tonight." He smiled, then scrubbed a hand across his forehead. "Or any night...of course."

They both laughed.

"Well, thank you." She relaxed a little. "You already know why I feel like a fish out of water. But why do you look so out of sorts tonight?"

He exhaled heavily, the frown returning to his face. "For one thing, I'd rather not be in the lineup. I'm doing this at my grandmother's insistence."

"Ms. Rose seems like a perfectly reasonable woman to me. And she loves you like crazy. I'm pretty sure if you'd turned her down she would've gotten over it fairly quickly."

"Maybe." He shrugged. "But the truth is that I owe my grandmother so much. Don't know where I would've ended up if it wasn't for her. Makes it hard to say no." A shadow of sadness passed over his handsome face, tugging at Tessa's heart.

Daniel had been raised by Rose Clayton after his own mother dumped him on her. It made Tessa's heart ache for him. She couldn't imagine the pain Daniel must feel at being abandoned by a woman who preferred drugs and booze to her own son.

"Of course." Tess nodded, regretting her earlier flippant words. She hadn't considered the special relationship that Daniel had with his grandmother and how grateful he must be to her. "I wasn't thinking."

They were both quiet for a moment, when she remembered his earlier words.

"You said 'for one thing.' What's the other reason you didn't want to do this?"

The pained look on Daniel's face carved deep lines in his forehead and between his brows. He drained the glass of whiskey in his hand.

"It's nothing," he said in a dismissive tone that made it clear that they wouldn't be discussing it any further.

She was digging herself deeper into a hole with every question she asked of Daniel tonight. Better for her to move on. She wished him luck and made her way over to the buffet table.

"Hey, Tessa." Lloyd Richardson put another slider on his small plate. "Wow, you look pretty amazing."

"Thanks, Lloyd." She decided against the slider and put some carrots and a cherry tomato on her plate instead.

There wasn't much room to spare in her fitted pantsuit. She wore a jacket over the sleeveless garment to hide the large cutout that revealed most of her back. That had been one idea of Rachel's for which she'd been grateful.

"Hey, you must be plum sick of people saying that to you by now." Lloyd seemed to recognize the discomfort she felt at all of the additional attention she'd been getting.

Tess gave him a grateful smile. No wonder her friend Gail Walker had a crush on Lloyd. He was handsome, sweet and almost a little shy. Which was probably why he hadn't made a move on Gail, since he certainly seemed interested in her.

"Okay, bachelors and bachelorette." Alexis acknowledged Tess with a slight smile. "The proceedings will begin in about ten minutes. So finish eating, take a quick bathroom break, whatever you need to do so you'll be ready to go on when your number is called."

Alexis had her serious, drill sergeant face on. Something Tessa knew firsthand that a woman needed to adopt when she was responsible for managing a crew of men—be they ranchers or ranch hands.

Still, there was something in her eyes. Had she been crying?

Before she could approach Alexis and ask if she was all right, she noticed the look Alexis and Daniel Clayton exchanged. It was brief, but meaningful. Chock full of pain.

Could Alexis be the other reason Daniel hadn't wanted to be in the bachelor auction? But from the look of things, whatever was going on between them certainly wasn't sunshine and roses.

Tessa caught up with Alexis as she grabbed the door handle.

"Alexis." Tessa lowered her voice as she studied her friend's face. "Is everything okay? You look like you've been—"

"I'm fine." Alexis swiped at the corner of one eye, her gaze cast downward. "I just... I'm fine." She forced a smile, finally raising her eyes to meet Tessa's. "You're going to kill them tonight. Just wait until you come out of that jacket. We're going to have to scrape everyone's jaws off the floor." She patted Tess's shoulder. "I'd tell you good luck, but something tells me that you aren't going to need it tonight."

With that, Alexis dipped out of the green room and was gone.

When Tess turned around, Daniel was standing there, staring after the other woman. He quickly turned away, busying himself with grabbing a bottle of water from the table.

There was definitely something going on with the two of them. And if there was, Tessa could understand why they wouldn't want to make their relationship public. Daniel's grandmother, Rose Clayton, and Alexis's grandfather, Gus Slade, once an item, had been feuding for years.

In recent months, they seemed to at least have found the civility to be decent toward one another. Most likely for the sake of everyone around them. Still, there was no love lost between those two families.

"Looks like Royal has its very own Romeo and Juliet," she muttered under her breath.

Tess took her seat, her hands trembling slightly and butterflies fluttering in her stomach. She closed her eyes, imagining how Ryan would react to seeing her out there on that stage.

Five

Ryan hung back at the bar as the bachelor auction wound down. There were just a couple more bachelors on the list, then Tess would be up.

He gulped the glass of water with lemon he was drinking. He'd talked to just about everyone here. But with neither Tripp nor Tess to hang out with, he'd been ready to leave nearly an hour ago.

Then again, his discomfort had little to do with him going stag for the night and everything to do with the fact that his best friend would be trotted out onto the stage and bid on. His gaze shifted around the garden at the unattached men in attendance. Most of them were members of the Texas Cattleman's Club. Some of them second, third or even fourth generation. All of them were good people, as far as he knew. So why was he assessing them all suspiciously? Wondering which of them would bid on his best friend.

The next bachelor, Lloyd Richardson, was called onto the stage and Alexis read his bio. Women were chomping at the bit to bid on the guy. Including Gail Walker. She'd started with a low, reasonable bid. But four or five other women were countering her bids as quickly as she was making them.

First the bid was in the hundreds, then the thousands. Suddenly, Steena Goodman, a wealthy older woman whose husband had been active in the club for many years before his death, stood and placed her final bid. Fifty-thousand dollars.

Ryan nearly coughed. What was it about this guy that had everyone up in arms?

Steena's bid was much higher than the previous bid of nine thousand dollars. The competing bidders pouted, acknowledging their defeat.

But not Gail. She looked angry and hurt. She stared Steena down, her arms folded and breathing heavily.

Alexis glanced back and forth at the two women for a moment. When Rachel nudged her, she cleared her throat and resumed her duties as auctioneer. "Going once, going twice—"

"One hundred thousand dollars." Gail stared at Steena, as if daring her to outbid her.

The older woman huffed and put her paddle down on the table, conceding the bid.

"Oh my God! One hundred thousand dollars." Alexis began the sentence nearly shrieking but ended with an implied question mark.

Probably because she was wondering the same thing he was.

Where in the hell did Gail Walker get that kind of cash?

Alexis declared Gail the winner of the bid at one hundred thousand dollars.

The woman squealed and ran up on stage. She wrapped her arms around Lloyd's neck and pulled him down for a hot, steamy kiss. Then she grabbed his hand and dragged him off the stage and through the doors that led from the garden back into the main building.

Ryan leaned against the bar, still shocked by Gail's outrageous bid. He sighed. Just one more bachelor, Daniel Clayton. Then Tess was up.

"That was certainly unexpected." Gus Slade ordered a beer from the bar. "Had no idea she was sitting on that kind of disposable cash."

"Neither did I, but I guess we all have our little secrets."

The older man grimaced, as if he'd taken exception to Ryan's words. Which only made Ryan wonder what secrets the old man might be hiding.

"Yes, well, I s'pose that's true." Gus nodded, then walked away.

Ryan turned his attention back to the stage just in time to see Daniel Clayton being whisked away excitedly by an overeager bidder.

There was a noticeable lull as Alexis watched the woman escort Daniel away. Rachel placed a hand on her cohost's back as she took the microphone from Alexis and thanked her for putting on a great event and being an incredible auctioneer.

Alexis seemed to recover from the momentarily stunned look she'd had seconds earlier. She nodded toward Rachel and then to the crowd which clapped appreciatively.

"This has been an amazing night, and thanks to your generosity, ladies, and to the generosity of our bachelors, we've already exceeded our fundraising goal for tonight. So thank you all for that. Give yourselves a big hand."

Rachel clapped a hand against the inside of her wrist as the rest of the audience clapped, hooted and shouted.

"But we're not done yet. It's time for the surprise you gents have been waiting for this evening. Fellas, please welcome our lone bachelorette, Miss Tessa Noble."

Ryan pulled out his phone. He'd promised Tripp that he'd record his sister's big debut.

There was a collective gasp in the room as Tessa stepped out onto the stage. Ryan moved away from the bar, so he could get a better view of his friend.

His jaw dropped, and his phone nearly clattered to the ground.

"Tess?" Ryan choked out the word, then silently cursed himself, realizing his stunned reaction would end up on the video. He snapped his gaping mouth shut as he watched her strut across the stage in a glamorous red pantsuit that seemed to be designed for the express purpose of highlighting her killer curves.

Damn, she's fine.

He wasn't an idiot. Nor was he blind. So he wasn't oblivious to the fact that his best friend also happened to be an extremely beautiful woman. And despite her tomboy wardrobe, he was fully aware of the hot body buried beneath relaxed fit clothing. But today…those curves had come out to play.

As if she was a professional runway model, Tess pranced to the end of the stage in strappy, glittery heels, put one hand on her hip and cocked it to the side. She seemed buoyed by the crowd's raucous reaction.

First there was the collective gasp, followed by a chorus of Oh my Gods. Now the crowd was whooping and shouting.

A slow grin spread across her lips, painted a deep, flirtatious shade of red that made him desperate to taste them. She turned and walked back toward where Rachel stood, revealing a large, heart-shaped cutout that exposed the warm brown skin of her open back. A large bow was tied behind her graceful neck.

Tessa Noble was one gift he'd give just about anything to unwrap.

She was incredibly sexy with a fiercely confident demeanor that only made him hunger for her more.

Ryan surveyed the crowd. He obviously wasn't the only man in the room drooling over Tessa 2.0. He stared at the large group of men who were wide-eyed, slack-jawed and obviously titillated by the woman on stage.

Tessa's concerns that no one would bid on her

were obviously misplaced. There were even a couple of women who seemed to be drooling over her.

Ryan's heart thudded. Suddenly, there wasn't enough air in the tented, outdoor space. He grabbed his auction paddle and crept closer to the stage.

Rachel read Tessa's bio aloud, as Alexis had done with the bachelors who'd gone before her. Tessa stood tall with her back arched and one hand on her hip. She held her head high as she scanned the room.

Was she looking for him?

Ryan's cheeks flushed with heat. A dozen emotions percolated in his chest, like some strange, volatile mixture, as he studied his friend on stage. Initially, he wanted to rush the stage and drape his jacket over her shoulders. Block the other men's lurid stares. Then there was his own guttural reaction to seeing Tess this way. He wanted to devour her. Kiss every inch of the warm, brown skin on her back. Glide his hands over her luscious bottom. Taste those pouty lips.

He swallowed hard, conscious of his rapid breathing. He hoped the video wasn't picking that up, too.

Rachel had moved on from Tessa's bio to describing her date. "For the lucky gentleman with the winning bid, your very special outing with this most lovely lady will be every man's fantasy come true. Your football-themed date will begin with seats on the fifty-yard line to watch America's team play football against their division rivals. Plus, you'll enjoy a special tailgating meal before the game at a restaurant right there in the stadium. Afterward, you'll share an elegant steak dinner at a premium steak house."

"Shit." Ryan cringed, realizing that, too, would be captured on the video.

There was already a stampede of overly eager men ready to take Tessa up on her offer. Now she'd gone and raised the stakes.

Just great.

Ryan huffed, his free hand clenched in a fist at his side, as her words reverberated through him.

You're only supposed to bid if no one else does.

Suddenly, Tessa's gaze met his, and her entire face lit up in a broad smile that made her even more beautiful. A feat he wouldn't have thought possible.

His heart expanded in his chest as he returned her smile and gave her a little nod.

Tess stood taller. As if his smile had lifted her. Made her even more confident.

And why shouldn't she be? She'd commanded the attention of every man in the room, single or not. Had all the women in the crowd enviously whispering among themselves.

"All right, gentlemen, get your paddles ready, because it's your turn to bid on our lovely bachelorette." Rachel grinned proudly.

He'd bet anything she was behind Tessa's incredible makeover. Ryan didn't know if he wanted to thank her or blame her for messing up a good thing. Back when no one else in town realized what a diamond his Tess was.

He shook his head. *Get it together, Bateman. She doesn't belong to you.*

"Shall we open the bidding at five-hundred dollars?" Rachel asked the crowd.

"A thousand dollars." Clem Davidson, a man his father's age, said.

"Fifteen hundred," Bo Davis countered. He was younger than Clem, but still much older than Tess.

Ryan clenched the paddle in his hand so tightly he thought it might snap in two as several of the men bid furiously for Tess. His heart thumped. Beads of sweat formed over his brow and trickled down his back as his gaze and the camera's shifted from the crowd of enthusiastic bidders to Tessa's shocked expression and then back again.

"Ten thousand bucks." Clem held his paddle high and looked around the room, as if daring anyone else to bid against him. He'd bid fifteen hundred dollars more than Bo's last bid.

Bo grimaced, but then nodded to Clem in concession.

"Twelve thousand dollars." It nearly came as a surprise to Ryan that the voice was his own.

Clem scowled. "Thirteen thousand."

"Fifteen thousand." Now Ryan's voice was the one that was indignant as he stared the older man down.

Clem narrowed his gaze at Ryan, his jaw clenched. He started to raise his paddle, but then his expression softened. Head cocked to the side, he furrowed his brows for a moment. Suddenly, he nodded to Ryan and put his paddle back down at his side.

"Fifteen thousand dollars going once. Fifteen thousand dollars going twice." Rachel looked around the room, excitedly. "Sold! Ryan Bateman, you may claim your bachelorette."

Ryan froze for a moment as everyone in the room looked at him, clapping and cheering. Many of them with knowing smiles. He cleared his throat, ended the recording and slowly made his way toward the stage and toward his friend who regarded him with utter confusion.

He stuffed his phone into his pocket, gave Tess an awkward hug and pressed a gentle kiss to her cheek for the sake of the crowd.

They all cheered, and he escorted Tess off the

stage. Then Rachel and Alexis wrapped up the auction.

"Oh my God, what did you just do?" Tessa whispered loudly enough for him to hear her over all the noise.

"Can't rightly say I know," he responded, not looking at her, but fully aware of his hand on her waist, his thumb resting on the soft skin of her back. Electricity sparked in his fingertips. Trailed up his arm.

"I appreciate what you did, Rye. It was a very generous donation. But I thought we agreed you would only bid if no one else did." Tessa folded her arms as she stared at him, searching his face for an answer.

"I know, and I was following the plan, I was. But I just couldn't let you go home with a guy like Clem."

Tessa stared up into his green eyes, her own eyes widening in response. Ryan Bateman was her oldest and closest friend. She knew just about everything there was to know about him. But the man standing before her was a mystery.

He'd gone beyond his usual protectiveness of her and had landed squarely into possessive territory. To be honest, it was kind of a turn-on. Which was problematic. Because Rye was her best friend. Emphasis on *friend*.

She folded her arms over her chest, suddenly self-conscious about whether the tightening of her nipples was visible through the thin material.

"And what, exactly, is it that you have against Clem?"

Ryan shook his head. "Nothing really." He seemed dazed, maybe even a little confused himself. "I just didn't want you to go out with him. He's too old for you."

"That's ageist." She narrowed her gaze.

It was true that she'd certainly never considered Clem Davidson as anything other than a nice older man. Still, it wasn't right for Ryan to single him out because of his age. It was a football date. Plain and simple. There would be no sex. With anyone.

"Clem isn't that much older than us, you know. Ten or fifteen years, tops." She relaxed her arms and ran her fingers through the silky waves that she still hadn't gotten accustomed to.

Ryan seemed to tense at the movement. He clenched his hand at his side, then nodded. "You're right on both counts. But what's done is done." He shrugged.

"What if it had been Bo instead? Would you have outbid him, too?"

"Yes." He seemed to regret his response, or at least the conviction with which he'd uttered the word. "I mean…yes," he said again.

"You just laid down fifteen grand for me," Tess said as they approached the bar. "The least I can do is buy you a drink."

She patted her hips, then remembered that her money and credit cards were in her purse backstage.

"Never mind. I've got it. Besides, I'm already running a tab." Ryan ordered a Jack and Coke for himself and one for her, which she turned down,

requesting club soda with lime instead. "You…
uh…you look pretty incredible."

"Thanks." She tried to sound grateful for the
compliment, but when everyone fawned over
how good she looked tonight, all she heard was
the implication that her everyday look was a hot
mess.

Her tomboy wardrobe had been a conscious
choice, beginning back in grade school. She'd de-
veloped early. Saw how it had changed the other
kids' perception of her. With the exception of
Ryan, the boys she'd been friends with were suddenly more fascinated with her budding breasts
than anything she had to say. And they'd come up
with countless ways to cop an "accidental" feel.

Several of the girls were jealous of her new-
found figure and the resulting attention from
the boys. They'd said hateful things to her and
started blatantly false rumors about her, which
only brought more unwanted attention from the
boys.

Tess had recognized, even then, that the problem was theirs, not hers. That they were imma-

ture and stupid. Still, it didn't stop the things they'd said from hurting.

She'd been too embarrassed to tell Tripp or Ryan, who were a few grades ahead of her. And she was worried that Ryan's temper would get him in serious trouble. She hadn't told her parents, either. They would've come to her school, caused a scene and made her even more of a social pariah.

So she'd worn bulky sweaters, loose jeans and flannel shirts that masked her curves and made her feel invisible.

After a while, she'd gotten comfortable in her wardrobe. Made it her own. Until it felt like her daily armor.

Wearing a seductive red pantsuit, with her entire back exposed and every curve she owned on display, made her feel as vulnerable as if she'd traipsed across the stage naked.

But she was glad she'd done it. That she'd reclaimed a little of herself.

The bartender brought their drinks and Ryan

stuffed a few dollars into the tip jar before taking a generous gulp of his drink.

"So, is this your new look?" An awkward smile lit Ryan's eyes. "'Cause it's gonna be mighty hard for you to rope a steer in that getup."

"Shut it, Rye." She pointed a finger at him, and they both laughed.

When they finally recovered from their laughter, she took his glass from his hand and took a sip of his drink. His eyes darkened as he watched her, his jaw tensing again.

"Not bad. Maybe I will have one." She handed it back to him.

Without taking his eyes off of her, Ryan signaled for the bartender to bring a Jack and Coke for her, too. There was something in his stare. A hunger she hadn't seen before.

She often longed for Ryan to see her as more than just "one of the boys." Now that it seemed he was finally seeing her that way, it was unsettling. His heated stare made her skin prickle with awareness.

The prospect of Ryan being as attracted to her

as she was to him quickened her pulse and sent a shock of warmth through her body. But just as quickly, she thought of how her relationship with the boys in school had changed once they saw her differently.

That wasn't something she ever wanted to happen between her and Ryan. She could deal with her eternal, unrequited crush, but she couldn't deal with losing his friendship.

She cleared her throat, and it seemed to break them both from the spell they'd both fallen under.

They were just caught up in emotions induced by the incredibly romantic setting, the fact that she looked like someone wholly different than her everyday self, and the adrenaline they'd both felt during the auction. Assigning it meaning... that would be a grave mistake. One that would leave one or both of them sorely disappointed once the bubble of illusion burst.

"So...since it's just us, we don't need to go out on a date. Because that would be...you know... weird. But, I'm totally down for hanging out. And seats on the fifty-yard line...so...yay."

"That's what I was really after." Ryan smirked, sipping his drink. "You could've been wearing a brown potato sack, and I still would've bid on those tickets. It's like the whole damned date had my name written all over it." His eyes widened with realization. "Wait…you did tailor it just for me, didn't you?"

Tessa's cheeks heated. She took a deep sip of her drink and returned it to the bar, waving a hand dismissively.

"Don't get ahead of yourself, partner. I simply used your tastes as a point of reference. After all, you, Tripp and my dad are the only men that I've been spending any significant time with these days. I figured if you'd like it, the bidders would, too."

"Hmm…" Ryan took another sip of his drink, almost sounding disappointed. "Makes sense, I guess."

"I'm glad you get it. Alexis and Rachel thought it was the least romantic thing they could imagine. They tried to talk me into something else. Something grander and more flowery."

"Which neither of us would've enjoyed." Ryan nodded. "And the makeover... I assume that was Rachel's idea, too."

"Both Alexis and Rachel came up with that one. Alexis got PURE to donate a spa day and the makeover, so it didn't cost me anything." Tessa tucked her hair behind her ear and studied her friend's face. "You don't like it?"

"No, of course I do. I love it. You look... incredible. You really do. Your parents are going to flip when they see this." He patted the phone in his pocket.

"You recorded it? Oh no." Part of her was eager to see the video. Another part of her cringed at the idea of watching herself prance across that stage using the catwalk techniques she'd studied online.

But no matter how silly she might feel right now, she was glad she'd successfully worked her magic on the crowd.

The opening chords of one of her favorite old boy band songs drew her attention to the stage where the band was playing.

"Oh my God, I love that song." Tessa laughed, sipping the last of her drink and then setting the glass on the bar. "Do you remember what a crush I had on these guys?"

Rye chuckled, regarding her warmly over the rim of his glass as he finished off his drink, too. "I remember you playing this song on repeat incessantly."

"That CD was my favorite possession. I still can't believe I lost it."

Ryan lowered his gaze, his chin dipping. He tapped a finger on the bar before raising his eyes to hers again and taking her hand. "I need to make a little confession."

"You rat!" She poked him in the chest. "You did something to my CD, didn't you?"

A guilty smirk curled the edges of his mouth. "Tripp and I couldn't take it anymore. We might've trampled the thing with a horse or two, then dumped it."

"You two are awful." She realized that she'd gone a little overboard in her obsession with the group. But trampling the album with a horse? That was harsh.

"If I'm being honest, I've always felt incredibly guilty about my role in the whole sordid affair." Ryan placed his large, warm hand on her shoulder. The tiny white lights that decorated the space were reflected in his green eyes. "Let me make it up to you."

"And just how do you plan to do that?" Tessa folded her arms, cocking a brow.

He pulled out his phone, swiped through a few screens. "First of all, I just ordered you another copy of that album—CD and digital."

She laughed. "You didn't need to do that, Rye."

"I did, and I feel much better now. Not just because it was wrong of us to take away something you loved so much. Because I hated having that secret between us all these years. You're the one person in the world I can tell just about anything. So it feels pretty damn good to finally clear my conscience." He dropped his hand from her shoulder.

"All right." She forced a smile, trying her best

to hide her disappointment at the loss of his touch. "And what's the second thing?"

He held his large, open palm out to her. "It seems I've bought myself a date for the night. Care to dance?"

"You want to dance to this sappy, boy band song that you've always hated?"

He grabbed her hand and led her to the dance floor. "Then I guess there's one more confession I need to make... I've always kind of liked this song. I just didn't want your brother to think I'd gone soft."

Tessa laughed as she joined her best friend on the dance floor.

Six

Gus Slade watched as Tessa Noble and Ryan Bateman entered the dance floor, both of them laughing merrily. Gus shook his head. Ryan was one of the prospects he'd considered as a good match for his granddaughter Alexis. Only it was clear that Ryan and Tess were hung up on each other, even if the self-proclaimed "best friends" weren't prepared to admit it to themselves.

It was no wonder Ryan's brief engagement to that wannabe supermodel he'd met in the city didn't last long enough for the two of them to make it to the altar.

Encouraging Alexis to start something with the Bateman boy would only result in heartache for his granddaughter once Ryan and Tess finally recognized the attraction flickering between them.

He'd experienced that kind of hurt and pain in his life when the woman he'd once loved, whom he thought truly loved him, had suddenly turned against him, shutting him out of her life.

It was something he'd never truly gotten over. Despite a long and happy marriage that lasted until the death of his dear wife.

Gus glanced over at Rose Clayton, his chest tightening. Even after all these years, the woman was still gorgeous. Just a hint of gray was visible at her temples. The rest of her hair was the same dark brown it was when she was a girl. She wore it in a stylish, modern cut that befit a mature woman. Yet, anyone who didn't know her could easily mistake her for a much younger woman.

And after all these years, Rose Clayton still turned heads, including his. The woman managed to stay as slim now as she had been back when she was a young girl. Yet, there was nothing weak or frail about Rose Clayton.

Her every move, her every expression, exuded a quiet confidence that folks around Royal had always respected. And tonight, he had to admit that she looked simply magnificent.

Gus glanced around the tented garden area again. The space looked glorious. Better than he could ever have imagined when the club first decided to undertake a major renovation of this space and a few other areas of the club, which had been in operation since the 1920s.

Alexis had headed up the committee that put on the auction. And his granddaughter had truly outdone herself.

Gus searched the crowd for Alexis. Her duties as Mistress of Ceremony appeared to be over for the night. Still, he couldn't locate her anywhere.

Gus walked toward the main building. Perhaps she was in the office or one of the other interior spaces. But as he looked through the glass pane, he could see Alexis inside, hemmed up by Daniel Clayton. From the looks of it, they were arguing.

Fists clenched at his sides, Gus willed himself to stay where he was rather than rushing inside and demanding that Daniel leave his granddaughter alone. If he did that, then Alexis would defend the boy.

That would defeat the purpose of the elaborate plan he and Rose Clayton had concocted to keep their grandkids apart.

So he'd wait there. Monitor the situation without interfering. He didn't want his granddaughter marrying any kin to Rose Clayton. Especially a boy with a mother like Stephanie Clayton. A heavy drinker who'd been in and out of trouble her whole life. A woman who couldn't be bothered to raise her own boy. Instead, she'd dumped him off on Rose who'd raised Daniel as if he was her own son.

From where he stood, it appeared that Daniel was pleading with Alexis. But she shoved his hand away when he tried to touch her arm.

Gus smirked, glad to see that someone besides him was getting the sharp end of that fierce stubborn streak she'd inherited from him.

Suddenly, his granddaughter threw her arms up and said something to Daniel that he obviously didn't like. Then she turned and headed his way.

Gus moved away from the door and around the corner to the bar as quickly and quietly as he could. He waited for her to pass by.

"Alexis!" Gus grabbed hold of her elbow as she hurried past him. He chuckled good-naturedly. "Where's the fire, darlin'?"

She didn't laugh. In fact, the poor thing looked dazed, like a wounded bird that had fallen out of the nest before it was time.

"Sorry, I didn't see you, Grandad." Her eyes didn't meet his. Instead, she looked toward the office where she was headed. "I'm sorry I don't have time to talk right now. I need to deal with a major problem."

"Alexis, honey, what is it? Is everything all right?"

"It will be, I'm sure. I just really need to take care of this now, okay?" Her voice trembled, seemed close to breaking.

"I wanted to tell you how proud I am of you.

Tonight was magnificent and you've raised so much money for pancreatic cancer research. Your grandmother would be so very proud of you."

Alexis suddenly raised her gaze to his, the corners of her eyes wet with tears. Rather than the intended effect of comforting her, his words seemed to cause her distress.

"Alexis, what's wrong?" Gus pleaded with his darling girl. The pain in her blue eyes, rimmed with tears, tore at his heart. "Whatever it is, you can talk to me."

Before she could answer, Daniel Clayton passed by. He and Alexis exchanged a long, painful look. Then Daniel dropped his gaze and continued to the other side of the room.

"Alexis, darlin', what's going on?"

The tears spilled from her eyes. Alexis sucked in a deep breath and sniffled.

"It's nothing I can't handle, Grandad." She wiped away the tears with brusque swipes of her hand and shook her head. "Thank you for everything you said. I appreciate it. Really. But

I need to take care of this issue. I'll see you back at home later, okay?"

Alexis pressed a soft kiss to his whiskered cheek. Then she hurried off toward the clubhouse offices.

Gus sighed, leaning against the bar. He dropped on to the stool, tapped the bar to get the bartender's attention, and ordered a glass of whiskey, neat. He gripped the hard, cold glass without moving it to his lips.

Their little plan was a partial success. Neither he nor Rose had been able to match their grandchildren up with an eligible mate. Yet, they'd done exactly what they'd set out to do. They'd driven a wedge between Daniel and Alexis.

So why didn't he feel good about what they'd done?

Because their grandkids were absolutely miserable.

What kind of grandfather could rejoice in the heartbreak of a beautiful girl like Alexis?

"Hello, Gus." Rose had sidled up beside him,

and ordered a white wine spritzer. "The kids didn't look too happy with each other just now."

"That's an understatement, if ever I've heard one." He gripped his glass and gulped from it. "They're in downright misery."

"Is it that bad?" She glanced over at him momentarily, studying his pained look, before accepting her glass of wine and taking a sip.

"Honestly? I think it's even worse." He scrubbed a hand down his jaw. "I feel like a heel for causing baby girl so much pain. And despite all our machinations, neither of us has found a suitable mate for our respective grandchildren."

She nodded sagely. Pain dimmed the light in her gray eyes. And for a moment, the shadow that passed over her lovely face made her look closer to her actual years.

"I'm sorry that they're both hurting. But it's better that they have their hearts broken now than to have it happen down the road, when they're both more invested in the relationship." She glanced at him squarely. "We've both known that pain.

It's a feeling that never leaves you. We're both living proof of that."

"I guess we are." Gus nodded, taking another sip of his whiskey. "But maybe there's something we hadn't considered." He turned around, his back to the bar.

"And what's that?" She turned on her bar stool, too, studying the crowd.

"Daniel and Alexis share our last names, but that doesn't make them us. And it doesn't mean they're doomed to our fates."

Rose didn't respond as she watched her grandson Daniel being fawned over by the woman who'd bought him at auction. He looked about as pleased by the woman's attentions as a man getting a root canal without anesthesia.

"We did what was in their best interests. The right thing isn't always the easiest thing. I know they're hurting now, but when they each find the person they were meant to be with, they'll be thankful this happened."

Rose paid for her drink and turned to walk away.

"Rose."

She halted, glancing over her shoulder without looking directly at him.

"What if the two of them were meant to be together? Will they be grateful we interfered then?"

A heavy sigh escaped her red lips, and she gathered her shawl around her before leaving.

His eyes trailed the woman as she walked away in a glimmering green dress. The dress was long, but formfitting. And despite her age, Rose was as tantalizing in that dress as a cool drink of water on a hot summer day.

After all these years he still had a thing for Rose Clayton. What if it was the same for Daniel and Alexis?

He ordered another whiskey, neat, hoping to God that he and Rose hadn't made a grave mistake they'd both regret.

Seven

Ryan twirled Tessa on the dance floor and then drew her back into his arms as they danced to one of his favorite upbeat country songs. Everyone around them seemed to be singing along with the lyrics which were both funny and slightly irreverent.

Tessa turned her back to him, threw her hands up, and wiggled her full hips as she sang loudly.

His attention was drawn to the sway of those sexy hips keeping time to the music. Fortunately, her dancing was much more impressive than her singing. Something his anatomy responded to, even if he didn't want it to. Particularly not while they were in the middle of a crowded dance floor.

Ryan swallowed hard and tried to shove away the rogue thoughts trying to commandeer his good sense. He and Tessa were just two friends enjoying their night together. Having a good time. *Nothing to see here, folks.*

"Everything okay?" Tessa had turned around, her beautiful brown eyes focused on him and a frown tugging down the corners of her mouth.

"Yeah, of course." He forced a smile. "I was just…thinking…that's all." He started to dance again, his movements forced and rigid.

Tessa regarded him strangely, but before she could probe further, Alexis appeared beside them looking flustered. Her eyes were red, and it looked like she'd been crying.

"Alexis, is something wrong?" Tessa turned to her friend and squeezed her hand.

"I'm afraid so. I've been looking everywhere for you two. Would you mind meeting with James and me in the office as soon as possible?" Alexis leaned in, so they could both hear her over the blaring music.

"Of course, we will." Tessa gave the woman's hand another assuring squeeze. "Just lead the way."

Alexis made her way through the crowd with Tessa and Ryan following closely behind.

Ryan bit back his disappointment at the interruption. If the distress Alexis appeared to be experiencing was any indication, the situation was one level below the barn being on fire. Which triggered a burning in his gut.

Whatever Alexis and James wanted with the two of them, he was pretty sure neither of them was going to like it.

"Tessa, Ryan, please, have a seat." James Harris, president of the Texas Cattleman's Club, gestured to the chairs on the other side of the large mahogany desk in his office.

After such a successful night, he and Alexis looked incredibly grim. The knot that had already formed in her gut tightened.

She and Ryan sat in the chairs James indicated while Alexis sat on the sofa along one wall.

"Something is obviously wrong." Ryan crossed one ankle over his knee. "What is it, James?"

The other man hesitated a moment before speaking. When he did, the words he uttered came out in an anguished growl.

"There was a problem with one of the bids. A *big* problem."

"Gail." Tessa and Ryan said her name simultaneously.

"How does something like this happen?" Ryan asked after James had filled them both in. "Can anyone just walk in off the street and bid a bogus hundred K?"

James grimaced.

Tessa felt badly for him. James hadn't been president of the Texas Cattleman's Club for very long. She could only imagine how he must be feeling. He'd been riding high after putting on what was likely the most successful fund-raiser in the club's history. But now he was saddled with one of the biggest faux pas in the club's history.

"It's a charity auction. We take folks at their word when they make a bid," James replied calmly, then sighed. "Still, I don't like that this happened on my watch, and I'll do everything I can to remedy the situation."

Tessa's heart broke for the man. She didn't know James particularly well, but she'd heard the tragic story about what had happened to his brother and his sister-in-law. They'd died in an accident, leaving behind their orphaned son, who was little more than a year old, to be raised by James.

He was a nice enough guy, but he didn't seem the daddy type. Still, he was obviously doing the best he could to juggle all the balls he had in the air.

Tessa groaned, her hand pressed to her forehead. "I knew Gail had a thing for Lloyd Richardson, but I honestly never imagined she'd do something so reckless and impulsive."

"No one thinks you knew anything about it, Tess. That's not why we asked you here," Alexis assured her.

"Then why are we here?" Ryan's voice was cautious as he studied the other man.

"Because we have another dilemma that could compound the first problem." James heaved a sigh as he sat back in his chair, his hands steepled over his abdomen. "And we could really use your help to head it off."

"Was there another bid that someone can't make good on?" Ryan asked.

"No, but there is a reporter here, whom I invited." Alexis cringed as she stood. "He's intrigued by that one-hundred thousand dollar bid, and he wants to interview Gail and Lloyd."

"Damn. I see your dilemma." Ryan groaned sympathetically. "Instead of getting good press about all of the money the club did raise, all anyone will be talking about is Gail and her bogus bid."

"It gets even worse," Alexis said. She blew out a frustrated breath as she shook her head, her blond locks flipping over her shoulder. "We can't find hide nor hair of either Gail or Lloyd. It's like the two of them simply vanished."

Ryan shook his head. "Wow. That's pretty messed up."

"What is it that you want Ryan and me to do?" Tessa looked at James and then Alexis.

"The reporter was also very intrigued by everyone's reaction to you and all the drama of how Ryan beat out Clem and Bo's bids." A faint smile flickered on Alexis's mouth. "So we suggested that he follow the two of you on your little date."

"What?"

Panic suddenly seized Tessa's chest. It was one thing to play dress up and strut on the stage here at the club. Surrounded mostly by people she'd known her entire life. It was another to be followed by a reporter who was going to put the information out there for the entire world to see.

"We hadn't really intended to go on a date," Tessa said. "Ryan and I were just going to hang out together and have fun at the game. Grab a bite to eat at his favorite restaurant. Nothing worthy of reporting on."

"I know." There was an apology in Alexis's

voice. "Which is why I need to ask another big favor…"

"You want us to go on a real date after all." Ryan looked from Alexis to James.

"Going out with a beautiful woman like Tess here, who also just happens to be your best friend…not the worst thing in the world that could happen to a guy." James forced a smile.

"Only…well, I know that the date you'd planned is the perfect kind of day for hanging with the guys." Alexis directed her attention toward Tess. "But this needs to feel like a big, romantic gesture. Something worthy of a big write-up for the event and for our club."

"I d-don't know, Alexis," Tessa stuttered, her heart racing. "I'm not sure how comfortable either of us would feel having a reporter follow us around all day."

"We'll do it," Ryan said suddenly. Decisively. "For the club, of course." He cleared his throat and gave Tess a reassuring nod. "And don't worry, I know exactly what to do. I'll make sure we give him the big, romantic fantasy he's looking for."

"I'm supposed to be the one who takes you out on a date," Tess objected. "That's how this whole thing works."

"Then it'll make for an even grander gesture when I surprise you by sweeping you off your feet."

He gave her that mischievous half smile that had enticed her into countless adventures. From searching for frogs when they were kids to parasailing in Mexico as an adult. After all these years, she still hadn't grown immune to its charm.

"Fine." Tessa sighed. "We'll do it. Just tell him we'll need a day or two to finalize the arrangements."

"Thank you!" Alexis hugged them both. "We're so grateful to you both for doing this."

"You're saving our asses here and the club's reputation." James looked noticeably relieved, though his eyebrows were still furrowed. "I can't thank you enough. And you won't be the only ones on the hot seat. Rose Clayton persuaded her grandson Daniel to give the reporter an additional positive feature related to the auction."

Alexis frowned at the mention of Daniel's name, but then she quickly recovered.

"And about that bid of Gail's…no one outside this room, besides Gail and Lloyd, of course, knows the situation." James frowned again. "We'd like to keep it that way until we figure out how we're going to resolve this. So please, don't whisper a word of this to anyone."

"Least of all the reporter," Alexis added, emphatically.

Tessa and Ryan agreed. Then Alexis introduced them to the reporter, Greg Halstead. After Greg gathered some preliminary information for the piece, Ryan insisted that he be the one to exchange contact information with Greg so they could coordinate him accompanying them on their date.

Every time Greg repeated the word *date*, shivers ran down Tessa's spine.

The only thing worse than having a thing for her best friend was being shanghaied into going on a fake date with him. But she was doing this for the club that meant so much to her, her family and the community of Royal.

Alexis had worked so hard to garner positive publicity for the club. And she'd raised awareness of the need to fund research for a cure for pancreatic cancer—the disease that had killed Alexis Slade's dear grandmother. Tess wouldn't allow all of her friend's hard work to be squandered because of Gail's selfish decision. Not if she could do something to prevent it.

Maybe she hadn't been aware of what Gail had planned to do tonight. But she'd been the one who'd invited Gail to tonight's affair. Tess couldn't help feeling obligated to do what she could to rectify the matter.

Even if it meant torturing herself by going on a pretend date that would feel very real to her. No matter how much she tried to deny it.

Eight

Ryan and Tessa finally headed home in his truck after what felt like an incredibly long night.

He couldn't remember the last time he and Tessa had danced together or laughed as much as they had that evening. But that was *before* James and Alexis had asked them to go on an actual date. Since then, things felt...different.

First, they'd politely endured the awkward interview with that reporter, Greg Halstead. Then they'd gone about the rest of the evening dancing and mingling with fellow club members and their guests. But there was a strange vibe between them. Obviously, Tessa felt it, too.

Why else would she be rambling on, as she often did when she was nervous.

Then again, lost in his own thoughts, he hadn't been very good company. Ryan drummed his fingers on the steering wheel during an awkward moment of silence.

"This date…it isn't going to make things weird between us, is it?" Tess asked finally, as if she'd been inside his head all along.

One of the hazards of a friendship with someone who knew him too well.

He forced a chuckle. "C'mon, Tess. We've been best buds too long to let a fake date shake us." His eyes searched hers briefly before returning to the road. "Our friendship could withstand anything."

Anything except getting romantically involved. Which is why they hadn't and wouldn't.

"Promise?" She seemed desperate for reassurance on the matter. Not surprising. A part of him needed it, too.

"On my life." This time, there was no hesitation. There were a lot of things in this world he could do without. Tessa Noble's friendship wasn't one of them.

Tessa nodded, releasing an audible sigh of relief. She turned to look out the window at the beautiful ranches that marked the road home.

His emphatic statement seemed to alleviate the anxiety they'd both been feeling. Still, his thoughts kept returning to their date the following weekend. The contemplative look on Tess's face, indicated that hers did, too.

He changed the subject, eager to talk about anything else. "What's up with your girl bidding a hundred K she didn't have?"

"I don't know." Tess seemed genuinely baffled by Gail's behavior.

Tessa and Gail certainly weren't as close as he and Tess were. But lately, at her mother's urging, Tessa had tried to build stronger friendships with other women in town.

She and Gail had met when Tessa had used the woman's fledgling grocery delivery business.

They'd hit it off and started hanging out occasionally.

He understood why Tess liked Gail. She was bold and a little irreverent. All of the things that Tess was not. But Ryan hadn't cared much for her. There was something about that woman he didn't quite trust. But now wasn't the time for I told you so's. Tessa obviously felt badly enough about being the person who'd invited Gail to the charity auction.

"I knew she had a lightweight crush on Lloyd Richardson," Tessa continued. "Who doesn't? But I certainly didn't think her capable of doing something this crazy and impulsive."

"Seems there was a lot of that going around," Ryan muttered under his breath.

"Speaking of that impulsiveness that seemed to be going around…" Tessa laughed, and Ryan chuckled, too.

He'd obviously uttered the words more to himself than to her. Still, she'd heard them, and they provided the perfect opening for what she'd been struggling to say all night.

"Thank you again for doing this, Rye. You made a very generous donation. And though you did the complete opposite of what I asked you to do—" they both laughed again "—I was a little… no, I was a *lot* nervous about going out with either Clem or Bo in such a high pressure situation, so thank you."

"Anything for you, Tess Noble." His voice was deep and warm. The emotion behind his words genuine. Something she knew from their history, not just as theory.

When they were in college, Ryan had climbed into his battered truck, and driven nearly two thousand miles to her campus in Sacramento after a particularly bad breakup with a guy who'd been an all-around dick. He'd dumped her for someone else a few days before Valentine's Day, so Ryan made a point of taking her to the Valentine's Day party. Then he kissed her in front of everyone—including her ex.

The kiss had taken her breath away. And left her wanting another taste ever since.

Tessa shook off the memory and focused on the here and now. Ryan had been uncharacteristically quiet during the ride home. He'd let her chatter on, offering a grunt of agreement or dissension here or there. Otherwise, he seemed deep in thought.

"And you're sure I can't pay you back at least some of what you bid on me?" Tessa asked as he slowed down before turning into the driveway of the Noble Spur, her family's ranch. "Especially since you're commandeering the planning of our date."

"Oh, we're still gonna use those tickets on the fifty-yard line, for sure," he clarified. "And there's no way I'm leaving Dallas without my favorite steak dinner. I'm just going to add some flourishes here and there. Nothing too fancy. But you'll enjoy the night. I promise." He winked.

Why did that small gesture send waves of electricity down her spine and make her acutely aware of her nipples prickling with heat beneath the jacket she'd put on to ward against the chilly night air?

"Well, thank you again," she said as he shifted his tricked out Ford Super Duty F-350 Platinum into Park. Ryan was a simple guy who didn't sweat the details—except when it came to his truck.

"You're welcome." Ryan lightly gripped her elbow when she reached for the door. "Allow me. Wouldn't want you to ruin that fancy outfit of yours."

He hopped out of the truck and came around to her side. He opened the door and took her hand.

It wasn't the first time Ryan had helped her out of his vehicle. But something about this time felt different. There was something in his intense green eyes. Something he wouldn't allow himself to say. Rare for a man who normally said just about anything that popped into his head.

When she stepped down onto the truck's side rail, Ryan released her hand. He gripped her waist and lifted her to the ground in a single deft move.

Tessa gasped in surprise, bracing her hands on

his strong shoulders. His eyes scanned her once more. As if he still couldn't believe it was really her in the sexiest, most feminine item of clothing she'd ever owned.

Heat radiated off his large body, shielding her from the chilliness of the night air and making her aware of how little space there was between them.

For a moment, the vision of Ryan's lips crashing down on hers as he pinned her body against the truck flashed through her brain. It wasn't an unfamiliar image. But, given their positions and the way he was looking at her right now, it felt a little too real.

Tessa took short, shallow breaths, her chest heaving. She needed to get away from Ryan Bateman before she did something stupid. Like lift on to her toes and press a hot, wet kiss to those sensual lips.

She needed to get inside and go to her room. The proper place to have ridiculously inappropriate thoughts about her best friend. With her battery-operated boyfriend buried in the nightstand drawer on standby, just in case she needed to take the edge off.

But walking away was a difficult thing to do when his mouth was mere inches from hers. And she trembled with the desire to touch him. To taste his mouth again. To trace the ridge behind the fly of his black dress pants.

"Good night." She tossed the words over her shoulder as she turned and headed toward the house as quickly as her feet would carry her in those high-heeled silver sandals.

"Tessa." His unusually gruff voice stopped her dead in her tracks.

She didn't turn back to look at him. Instead, she glanced just over her shoulder. A sign that he had her full attention, even if her eyes didn't meet his. "Yes?"

"I'm calling an audible on our date this weekend." Ryan invoked one of his favorite football terms.

"A last-minute change?" Tessa turned slightly, her curiosity piqued.

She'd planned the perfect weekend for Ryan Bateman. What could she possibly have missed?

"I'll pick you up on Friday afternoon, around 3:00 p.m. Pack a bag for the weekend. And don't forget that jumpsuit."

"We're spending the entire weekend in Dallas?" She turned to face him fully, stunned by the hungry look on his face. When he nodded his confirmation, Tessa focused on slowing her breath as she watched the cloud her warm breath made in the air. "Why? And since when do you care what I wear?"

"Because I promised Alexis I'd make this date a big, grand gesture that would keep the reporter preoccupied and off the topic of our missing bachelor and his hundred-thousand-dollar bidder." His words were matter of fact, signaling none of the raw, primal heat she'd seen in his eyes a moment ago.

He shut the passenger door and walked around to the driver's side. "It doesn't have to be that same outfit. It's just that you looked mighty pretty tonight. Neither of us gets much of a chance to dress up. Thought it'd be nice if we took advantage of this weekend to do that." He shrugged, as if it were the most normal request in the world.

This coming from a man who'd once stripped out of his tuxedo in the car on the way home from a mutual friend's out-of-town wedding. He'd insisted he couldn't stand to be in that tuxedo a moment longer.

"Fine." Tessa shrugged, too. If it was no big deal to Ryan, then it was no big deal to her either. "I'll pack a couple of dresses and skirts. Maybe I'll wear the dress I'd originally picked out for tonight. Before I volunteered to be in the auction."

After all that waxing, she should show her baby smooth legs off every chance she got. Who knew when she'd put herself through that kind of torture again?

"Sounds like you got some packing to do." A restrained smirk lit Ryan's eyes. He nodded toward the house. "Better get inside before you freeze out here."

"'Night, Ryan." Tessa turned up the path to the house, without waiting for his response, and let herself in, closing the door behind her. The slam of the heavy truck door, followed by the crunch of gravel, indicated that Ryan was turning his vehicle around in the drive and heading home to the Bateman Ranch next door.

Tessa released a long sigh, her back pressed to the door.

She'd just agreed to spend the weekend in Dallas with her best friend. Seventy-two hours of pretending she didn't secretly lust after Ryan Bateman. Several of which would be documented by a reporter known for going after gossip.

Piece of cake. Piece of pie.

Nine

"Tessa, your chariot is here," Tripp called to her upstairs. "Hurry up, you're not gonna believe this."

Tripp was definitely back to his old self. It was both a blessing and a curse, because he hadn't stopped needling her and Ryan about their date ever since.

She inhaled deeply, then slowly released the breath as she stared at herself in the mirror one last time.

It's just a weekend trip with a friend. Ryan and I have done this at least a dozen times before. No big deal.

Tessa lifted her bag on to her shoulder, then made her way downstairs and out front where Tripp was handing her overnight suitcase off to Ryan.

Her eyes widened as she walked closer, studying the sleek black sedan with expensive black rims.

"Is that a black on black Maybach?"

"It is." Ryan took the bag from her and loaded it into the trunk of the Mercedes Maybach before closing it and opening the passenger door. He gestured for her to get inside. "You've always said you wanted to know what it was like to ride in one of these things, so—"

"You didn't go out and buy this, did you?" Panic filled her chest. Ryan wasn't extravagant or impulsive. And he'd already laid out a substantial chunk of change as a favor to her.

"No, of course not. You know a mud-caked pickup truck is more my style." He leaned in and lowered his voice, so only she could hear his next words. "But I'm supposed to be going for the entire illusion here, remember? And Tess…"

"Yes?" She inhaled his clean, fresh scent, her heart racing slightly from his nearness and the intimacy of his tone.

"Smile for the camera." Ryan nodded toward Greg Halstead who waved and snapped photographs of the two of them in front of the vehicle.

Tess deepened her smile, and she and Ryan stood together, his arm wrapped around her as the man clicked photos for the paper.

When Greg had gotten enough images, he shook their hands and said he'd meet them at the hotel later and at the restaurant tomorrow night to get a few more photos.

"Which hotel? And which restaurant?" Tessa turned to Ryan.

A genuine smile lit his green eyes and they sparkled in the afternoon sunlight. "If I tell you, it won't be a surprise, now will it?"

"Smart-ass." She folded her arms and shook her head. Ryan knew she liked surprises about as much as she liked diamondback rattlesnakes. Maybe even a little less.

"There anything I should know about you

two?" Tripp stepped closer after the reporter was gone. Arms folded over his chest, his gaze shifted from Ryan to her and then back again.

"You can take the protective big brother shtick down a notch," she teased. "I already explained everything to you. We're doing this for the club, and for Alexis."

She flashed her I'm-your-little-sister-and-you-love-me-no-matter-what smile. It broke him. As it had for as long as she could remember.

The edge of his mouth tugged upward in a reluctant grin. He opened his arms and hugged her goodbye before giving Ryan a one-arm bro hug and whispering something to him that she couldn't hear.

Ryan's expression remained neutral, but he nodded and patted her brother on the shoulder.

"We'd better get going." Ryan helped her into the buttery, black leather seat that seemed to give her a warm hug. Then he closed her door and climbed into the driver's seat.

"God, this car is beautiful," she said as he

pulled away from the house. "If you didn't buy it, whose is it?

"Borrowed it from a friend." He pulled on to the street more carefully than he did when he was driving his truck. "The guy collects cars the way other folks collect stamps or Depression-era glass. Most of the cars he wouldn't let anyone breathe on, let alone touch. But he owed me a favor."

Tessa sank back against the seat and ran her hand along the smooth, soft leather.

"Manners would dictate that I tell you that you shouldn't have, but if I'm being honest, all I can think is, Where have you been all my life?" They both chuckled. "You think I can have a saddle made out of this leather?"

"For the right price, you can get just about anything." A wide smile lit his face.

Tessa sighed. She was content. Relaxed. And Ryan seemed to be, too. There was no reason this weekend needed to be tense and awkward.

"So, what did my brother say to you when he gave you that weird bro hug goodbye?"

The muscles in Ryan's jaw tensed and his brows furrowed. He kept his gaze on the road ahead. "This thing has an incredible sound system. I already synced it to my phone. Go ahead and play something. Your choice. Just no more '80s boy bands. I heard enough of those at the charity auction last week."

Tessa smirked. "You could've just told me it was none of my business what Tripp said."

His wide smile returned, though he didn't look at her. "I thought I just did."

They both laughed, and Tessa smiled to herself. Their weekend was going to be fun. Just like every other road trip they'd ever taken together. Things would only be uncomfortable between them if she made them that way.

Ryan, Tessa and Greg Halstead headed up the stone stairs that led to the bungalow of a fancy, art-themed boutique hotel that he'd reserved. The place was an easy drive from the football stadium.

Tessa had marveled at the hotel's main building and mused about the expense. But she was as excited as a little kid in a candy store, eager to see what was on the other side of that door. Greg requested to go in first, so he could set up his shot of Tessa stepping inside the room.

When he signaled that he was ready, Ryan inserted the key card into the lock and removed it quickly. Once the green light flashed, he opened the door for her.

Tessa's jaw dropped, and she covered her mouth with both hands, genuinely stunned by the elegant beauty of the contemporary bungalow.

"So…what do you think?" He couldn't shake the nervousness he felt. The genuine need to impress her was not his typical MO. So what was going on? Maybe it was the fact that her impression would be recorded for posterity.

"It's incredible, Ryan. I don't know what to say." Her voice trembled with emotion. When she glanced up at him, her eyes were shiny. She wiped quickly at the corners of her eyes. "I'm being silly, I know."

"No, you're not." He kissed her cheek. "That's exactly the reaction I was hoping for."

Ryan stepped closer and lowered his voice. "I want this to be a special weekend for you, Tess. What you did last week at the charity auction was brave, and I'm proud of you. I want this weekend to be everything the fearless woman who strutted across that stage last Saturday night deserves."

His eyes met hers for a moment and his chest filled with warmth.

"Thanks, Rye. This place is amazing. I really appreciate everything you've done." A soft smile curled the edges of her mouth, filling him with the overwhelming desire to lean down and kiss her the way he had at that Valentine's Day party in college.

He stepped back and cleared his throat, indicating that she should step inside.

Tessa went from room to room of the two-bedroom, two-bath hotel suite, complete with two balconies. One connected to each bedroom. There was even a small kitchen island, a full-size refrigerator and a stove. The open living room boasted a ridiculously large television mounted to the wall and a fireplace in both that space and the master bedroom, which he insisted that she take. But Tessa, who could be just as stubborn as he was, wouldn't hear of it. She directed the bellman to take her things to the slightly smaller bedroom, which was just as beautiful as its counterpart.

"I think I have all the pictures I need." Greg gathered up his camera bag and his laptop. "I'll work on the article tonight and select the best photos among the ones I've taken so far. I'll meet you guys at the restaurant tomorrow at six-thirty to capture a few more shots."

"Sounds good." Ryan said goodbye to Greg and closed the door behind him, glad the man was finally gone. Something about a reporter hanging around, angling for a juicy story, felt like a million ants crawling all over his skin.

He sank on to the sofa, shrugged his boots off, and put his feet up on the coffee table. It'd been a short drive from Royal to Dallas, but mentally, he was exhausted.

Partly from making last-minute arrangements for their trip. Partly from the effort of reminding himself that no matter how much it felt like it, this wasn't a real date. They were both just playing their parts. Making the TCC look good and diverting attention from the debacle of Gail's bid.

"Hey." Tess emerged from her bedroom where she'd gone to put her things away. "Is Greg gone?"

"He left a few minutes ago. Said to tell you goodbye."

"Thank goodness." She heaved a sigh and plopped down on the sofa beside him. "I mean, he's a nice guy and everything. It just feels so... I don't know..."

"Creepy? Invasive? Weird?" he offered. "Take your pick."

"All of the above." Tessa laughed, then leaned forward, her gaze locked on to the large bouquet of flowers in a glass vase on the table beside his feet.

"I thought these were just part of the room." She removed the small envelope with her name on it and slid her finger beneath the flap, prying it open. "These are for me?"

"I hope you like them. They're—"

"Peonies. My favorite flower." She leaned forward and inhaled the flowers that resembled clouds dyed shades of light and dark pink. "They're beautiful, Ryan. Thank you. You thought of everything, didn't you?" Her voice trailed and her gaze softened.

"I meant it when I said you deserve a really special weekend. I even asked them to stock the freezer with your favorite brand of Neapolitan ice cream."

"Seriously?" She was only wearing a hint of lip gloss in a nude shade of pink and a little eyeshadow and mascara. But she was as beautiful as he'd ever seen her. Even more so than the night of the auction when she'd worn a heavy layer of makeup that had covered her creamy brown skin. Sunlight filtered into the room, making her light brown eyes appear almost golden. "What more could I possibly ask for?"

His eyes were locked on her sensual lips. When

he finally tore his gaze away from them, Tess seemed disappointed. As if she'd expected him to lean in and kiss her.

"I like the dress, by the way."

"Really?" She stood, looking down at the heather-gray dress and the tan calf-high boots topped by knee socks. The cuff of the socks hovered just above the top of the boot, drawing his eye there and leading it up the side of her thigh where her smooth skin disappeared beneath the hem of her dress.

His body stiffened in response to her curvy silhouette and her summery citrus scent.

Fucking knee socks. *Seriously?* Tess was *killing* him.

For a moment he wondered if she was teasing him on purpose. Reminding him of the things he couldn't have with her. The red-hot desires that would never be satisfied.

Tess seemed completely oblivious to her effect on him as she regarded the little gray dress.

Yet, all he could think of was how much he'd

like to see that gray fabric pooled on the floor beside his bed.

Ryan groaned inside. This was going to be the longest seventy-two hours of his life.

Ten

"Is that a bottle of champagne?" Tessa pointed to a bottle chilling in an ice bucket on the sideboard along the wall.

She could use something cold to tamp down the heat rising in her belly under Ryan's intense stare. It also wouldn't be a bad idea to create some space between them. Enough to get her head together and stop fantasizing about what it would feel like to kiss her best friend again.

"Even better." Ryan flashed a sexy, half grin. "It's imported Italian Moscato d'Asti. I asked them to chill a bottle for us."

Her favorite. Too bad this wasn't a real date, because Ryan had ticked every box of what her fantasy date would look like.

"Saving it for something special?"

"Just you." He winked, climbing to his feet. "Why don't we make a toast to kick our weekend off?"

Tessa relaxed a little as she followed him over to the ice bucket, still maintaining some distance between them.

Ryan opened the bottle with a loud pop and poured each of them a glass of the sparkling white wine. He handed her one.

She accepted, gratefully, and joined him in holding up her glass.

"To an unforgettable weekend." A soft smile curved the edges of his mouth.

"Cheers." Tessa ignored the beading of her nipples and the tingling that trailed down her spine and sparked a fire low in her belly. She took a deep sip.

"Very good." Tessa fought back her speculation about how much better it would taste on Ryan's lips.

Ryan returned to the sofa. He finished his glass of moscato in short order and set it on the table beside the sofa.

Tessa sat beside him, finishing the remainder of her drink and contemplating another. She decided against it, setting it on the table in front of them.

She turned to her friend. God, he was handsome. His green eyes brooding and intense. His shaggy brown hair living in that space between perfectly groomed and purposely messy. The ever-present five o'clock shadow crawling over his clenched jaw.

"Thanks, Rye." She needed to quell the thoughts in her head. "This is all so amazing and incredibly thoughtful. I know this fantasy date isn't real, but you went out of your way to make it feel that way, and I appreciate it."

Tessa leaned in to kiss his stubbled cheek. Something she'd done a dozen times before. But Ryan turned his head, likely surprised by her sudden approach, and her lips met his.

She'd been right. The moscato did taste better enmeshed with the flavor of Ryan's firm, sensual lips.

It was an accidental kiss. So why had she leaned in and continued to kiss him, rather than withdrawing and apologizing? And why hadn't Ryan pulled back either?

Tessa's eyes slowly drifted closed, and she slipped her fingers into the short hair at the nape of Ryan's neck. Pulled his face closer to hers.

She parted her lips, and Ryan accepted the unspoken invitation, sliding his tongue between her lips and taking control. The kiss had gradually moved from a sweet, inadvertent, closed-mouth affair to an intense meshing of lips, teeth and tongues. Ryan moved his hands to her back, tugging her closer.

Tessa sighed softly in response to the hot, demanding kiss that obliterated the memory of that unexpected one nearly a decade ago. Truly kissing Ryan Bateman was everything she'd imagined it to be.

And she wanted more.

They'd gone this far. Had let down the invisible wall between them. There was nothing holding them back now.

Tessa inhaled deeply before shifting to her knees and straddling Ryan's lap. He groaned. A sexy sound that was an undeniable mixture of pain and pleasure. Of intense wanting. Evident from the ridge beneath his zipper.

As he deepened their kiss, his large hand splayed against her low back, his hardness met the soft, warm space between her thighs, sending a shiver up her spine. Her nipples ached with an intensity she hadn't experienced before. She wanted his hands and lips on her naked flesh. She wanted to shed the clothing that prevented skin-to-skin contact.

She wanted…sex. With Ryan. Right now.

Sex.

It wasn't as if she'd forgotten how the whole process worked. Obviously. But it'd been a while since she'd been with anyone. More than a few years. One of the hazards of living in a town small enough that there was three degrees or less of separation between any man she met and her father or brother.

Would Ryan be disappointed?

Tessa suddenly went stiff, her eyes blinking.

"Don't," he whispered between hungry kisses along her jaw and throat that left her wanting and breathless, despite the insecurities that had taken over her brain.

Tess frowned. "Don't do what?"

Maybe she didn't have Ryan Bateman's vast sexual experience, but she was pretty sure she knew how to kiss. At least she hadn't had any complaints.

Until now.

"Have you changed your mind about this?"

"No." She forced her eyes to meet his, regardless of how unnerved she was by his intense stare and his determination to make her own up to what she wanted. "Not even a little."

The edge of his mouth curved in a criminally sexy smirk. "Then for once in your life, Tess, stop overthinking everything. Stop compiling a list in your head of all the reasons we shouldn't do this." He kissed her again, his warm lips pressed to hers and his large hands gliding down her back and gripping her bottom as he pulled her firmly against him.

A soft gasp escaped her mouth at the sensation of his hard length pressed against her sensitive flesh. Ryan swept his tongue between her parted lips, tangling it with hers as he wrapped his arms around her.

Their kiss grew increasingly urgent. Hungry. Desperate. His kiss made her question whether she'd ever *really* been kissed before. Made her skin tingle with a desire so intense she physically ached with a need for him.

A need for Ryan's kiss. His touch. The warmth of his naked skin pressed against hers. The feel of him inside her.

Hands shaking and the sound of her own heartbeat filling her ears, Tessa pulled her mouth from his. She grabbed the hem of her dress and raised it. His eyes were locked with hers, both of them breathing heavily, as she lifted the fabric.

Ryan helped her tug the dress over her head

and he tossed it on to the floor. He studied her lacy, gray bra and the cleavage spilling out of it.

Her cheeks flamed, and her heart raced. Ryan leaned in and planted slow, warm kisses on her shoulder. He swept her hair aside and trailed kisses up her neck.

"God, you're beautiful, Tess." His voice was a low growl that sent tremors through her. He glided a callused hand down her back and rested it on her hip. "I think it's pretty obvious how much I want you. But I need to know that you're sure about this."

"I am." She traced his rough jaw with her palm. Glided a thumb across his lips, naturally a deep shade of red that made them even more enticing. Then she crashed her lips against his as she held his face in her hands.

He claimed her mouth with a greedy, primal kiss that strung her body tight as a bow, desperate for the release that only he could provide.

She wanted him. More than she could ever remember wanting anything. The steely rod pressed against the slick, aching spot between her thighs indicated his genuine desire for her. Yet, he seemed hesitant. As if he were holding back. Something Ryan Bateman, one of the most confident men she'd ever known, wasn't prone to do.

Tess reached behind her and did the thing Ryan seemed reluctant to. She released the hooks on her bra, slid the straps down her shoulders and tossed it away.

He splayed one hand against her back. The other glided up and down her side before his thumb grazed the side of her breast. Once, twice, then again. As if testing her.

Finally, he grazed her hardened nipple with his open palm, and she sucked in a sharp breath.

His eyes met hers with a look that fell somewhere between asking and pleading.

Tessa swallowed hard, her cheeks and chest flushed with heat. She nodded, her hands trembling as she braced them on his wide shoulders.

When Ryan's lips met her skin again, she didn't fight the overwhelming feelings that flooded her senses, like a long, hard rain causing the creek to exceed its banks. She leaned into them. Allowed them to wash over her. Enjoyed the thing she'd fantasized about for so long.

Tessa gasped as Ryan cupped her bottom and pulled her against his hardened length. As if he was as desperate for her as she was for him. He kissed her neck, her shoulders, her collarbone. Then he dropped tender, delicate kisses on her breasts.

Tessa ran her fingers through his soft hair. When he raised his eyes to hers, she leaned down, whispering in his ear.

"Ryan, take me to bed. Now."

Before she lost her nerve. Before he lost his.

Ryan carried her to his bed, laid her down and settled between her thighs. He trailed slow, hot kisses down her neck and chest as he palmed her breast with his large, work-roughened hand. He sucked the beaded tip into his warm mouth. Grazed it with his teeth. Lathed it with his tongue.

She shuddered in response to the tantalizing sensation that shot from her nipple straight to her sex. Her skin flamed beneath Ryan's touch, and her breath came in quick little bursts. He nuzzled her neck, one large hand skimming down her thigh and hooking behind her knee. As he rocked against the space between her thighs, Tessa whimpered at the delicious torture of his steely length grinding against her needy clit.

"That's it, Tess." Ryan trailed kisses along her jaw. "Relax. Let go. You know I'd never do anything to hurt you." His stubble scraped the sensitive skin of her cheek as he whispered roughly in her ear.

She did know that. She trusted Ryan with her life. With her deepest secrets. With her body. Ryan was sweet and charming and well-meaning, but her friend could sometimes be a bull in the china shop.

Would he ride roughshod over her heart, even if he didn't mean to?

Tessa gazed up at him, her lips parting as she took in his incredibly handsome form. She yanked his shirt from the back of his pants and slid her hands against his warm skin. Gently grazed his back with her nails. She had the fleeting desire to mark him as hers. So that any other woman who saw him would know he belonged to her and no one else.

Ryan moved beside her, and she immediately missed his weight and the feel of him pressed against her most sensitive flesh. He kissed her harder as he slid a hand up her thigh and then cupped the space between her legs that throbbed in anticipation of his touch.

Tessa tensed, sucking in a deep breath as he glided his fingertips back and forth over the drenched panel of fabric shielding her sex. He tugged the material aside and plunged two fingers inside her.

"God, you're wet, Tess." The words vibrated against her throat, where he branded her skin with scorching hot kisses that made her weak with want. He kissed his way down her chest and gently scraped her sensitive nipple with his teeth before swirling his tongue around the sensitive flesh.

Tessa quivered as the space between her thighs ached with need. She wanted to feel him inside her. To be with Ryan in the way she'd always imagined.

But this wasn't a dream; it was real. And their actions would have real-world consequences.

"You're doing it again. That head thing," he muttered in between little nips and licks. His eyes glinted in the light filtering through the bedroom window. "Cut it out."

God, he knew her too well. And after tonight, he would know every single inch of her body. If she had her way.

Eleven

Ryan couldn't get over how beautiful Tessa was as she lay beside him whimpering with pleasure. Lips parted, back arched and her eyelashes fluttering, she was everything he'd imagined and more.

He halted his action just long enough to encourage her to lift her hips, allowing him to drag the lacy material down her legs, over her boots, and off. Returning his attention to her full breasts, he sucked and licked one of the pebbled, brown peaks he'd occasionally glimpsed the outline of through the thin, tank tops she sometimes wore during summer. He'd spent more time than he dared admit speculating about what her breasts looked like and how her skin would taste.

Now he knew. And he desperately wanted to know everything about her body. What turned her on? What would send her spiraling over the edge, his name on her lips?

He eagerly anticipated solving those mysteries, too.

Ryan inserted his fingers inside her again, adding a third finger to her tight, slick channel. Allowed her body to stretch and accommodate the additional digit.

He and Tess had made it a point not to delve too deeply into each other's sex lives. Still, they'd shared enough for him to know he wouldn't be her first or even her second. She was just a little tense, and perhaps a lot nervous. And she needed to relax.

Her channel stretched and relaxed around his fingers as he moved to her other nipple and gave it the same treatment he'd given the first. He resumed the movement of his hand, his fingers gliding in and out of her. Then he stroked the slick bundle of nerves with his thumb.

Tessa's undeniable gasp of pleasure indicated her approval.

The slow, small circles he made with his thumb got wider, eliciting a growing chorus of curses and moans. Her grip on his hair tightened, and she moved her hips in rhythm with his hand.

She was slowly coming undone, and he was grateful to be the reason for it. Ryan wet his lips with a sweep of his tongue, eager to taste her there. But he wanted to take his time. Make this last for both of them.

He kissed Tessa's belly and slipped his other hand between her legs, massaging her clit as he curved the fingers inside her.

"Oh god, oh god, oh god, Ryan. Right there, right there," Tess pleaded when he hit the right spot.

He gladly obliged her request, both hands moving with precision until he'd taken Tess to the edge. She'd called his name, again and again, as she dug the heels of her boots into the mattress and her body stiffened.

Watching his best friend tumble into bliss was a thing of beauty. Being the one who'd brought her such intense ecstasy was an incredible gift. It was easily the most meaningful sexual experience he'd ever had, and he was still fully clothed.

Ryan lay down, gathering Tess to him and wrapping her in his arms, her head tucked under his chin. He flipped the cover over her, so she'd stay warm.

They were both silent. Tessa's chest heaved as she slowly came down from the orgasm he'd given her.

When the silence lingered on for seconds that turned to minutes, but felt like hours, Ryan couldn't take it.

"Tess, look, I—"

"You're still dressed." She raised her head, her eyes meeting his. Her playful smile eased the tension they'd both been feeling. "And I'm not quite sure why."

The laugh they shared felt good. A bit of normalcy in a situation that was anything but normal between them.

He planted a lingering kiss on her sweet lips.

"I can fix that." He sat up and tugged his shirt over his head and tossed it on to the floor unceremoniously.

"Keep going." She indicated his pants with a wave of her hand.

"Bold and bossy." He laughed. "Who is this woman and what did she do with my best friend?"

She frowned slightly, as if what he'd said had hurt her feelings.

"Hey." He cradled her face in one hand. "You know that's not a criticism, right? I like seeing this side of you."

"Usually when a man calls a woman bossy, it's code for bitchy." Her eyes didn't quite meet his.

Ryan wanted to kick himself. He'd only been teasing when he'd used the word bossy, but he hadn't been thinking. He understood how loaded that term was to Tess. She'd hated that her mother and grandmother had constantly warned her that no ranch man would want a bossy bride.

"I should've said assertive," he clarified. "Which is what I've always encouraged you to be."

She nodded, seemingly satisfied with his explanation. A warm smile slid across her gorgeous face and lit her light brown eyes. "Then I'd like to assert that you're still clothed, and I don't appreciate it, seeing as I'm not."

"Yes, ma'am." He winked as he stood and removed his pants.

Tessa gently sank her teeth into her lower lip as she studied the bulge in his boxer briefs. Which only made him harder.

He rubbed the back of his neck and chuckled. "Now I guess I know how the fellas felt on stage at the auction."

"Hmm..." The humming sound Tess made seemed to vibrate in his chest and other parts of his body. Specifically, the part she was staring at right now.

Tess removed her boots and kneeled on the bed in front of him, her brown eyes studying him. The levity had faded from her expression, replaced by a heated gaze that made his cock twitch.

She looped her arms around his neck and pulled his mouth down toward hers. Angling her head, she kissed him hard, her fingers slipping into his hair and her naked breasts smashed against his hard chest.

If this was a dream, he didn't want to wake up.

Ryan wrapped his arms around Tess, needing her body pressed firmly against his. He splayed one hand against the smooth, soft skin of her back. The other squeezed the generous bottom he'd always quietly admired. Hauling her tight against him, he grew painfully hard with the need to be inside her.

He claimed her mouth, his tongue gliding against hers, his anticipation rising. He'd fanta-sized about making love to Tess long before that kiss they'd shared in college.

He'd wanted to make love to her that night. Or at the very least make out with her in his truck. But he'd promised Tripp he wouldn't ever look at Tess that way.

A promise he'd broken long before tonight, despite his best efforts.

Ryan pushed thoughts of his ill-advised pledge to Tripp and the consequences of breaking it from his mind.

Right now, it was just him and Tess. The only thing that mattered in this moment was what the two of them wanted. What they needed from each other.

Ryan pulled away, just long enough to rummage in his luggage for the condoms he kept in his bag.

He said a silent prayer, thankful there was one full strip left. He tossed it on the nightstand and stripped out of his underwear.

Suddenly she seemed shy again as his eyes roved every inch of her gorgeous body.

He placed his hands on her hips, pulling her close to him and pressing his forehead to hers.

"God, you're beautiful, Tess." He knew he sounded like a broken record. But he was struck by how breathtaking she was and by the fact that she'd trusted him with something as precious as her body.

"You're making me feel self-conscious." A deep blush stained Tess's cheeks and spread through her chest.

"Don't be." He cradled her cheek, hoping to put her at ease. "That's not my intention. I just…" He sighed, giving up on trying to articulate what he was feeling.

One-night stands, even the occasional relationship…those were easy. But with Tess, everything felt weightier. More significant. Definitely more complicated. He couldn't afford to fuck this up. Because not having Tess as his friend wasn't an option. Still, he wanted her.

"Ryan, it's okay." She wrapped her arms around him. "I'm nervous about this, too. But I know that I want to be with you tonight. It's what I've wanted for a long time, and I don't want to fight it anymore."

He shifted his gaze to hers. A small sigh of relief escaped his mouth.

Tess understood exactly what he was feeling.

They could do this. Be together like this. Satisfy their craving for each other without ruining their friendship.

He captured her mouth in a bruising kiss, and they both tumbled on to the mattress. Hands groping. Tongues searching. Hearts racing.

He grabbed one of the foil packets and ripped it open, sheathing himself as quickly as he could.

He guided himself to her slick entrance, circling his hips so his pelvis rubbed against her hardened clit. Tessa gasped, then whimpered with pleasure each time he ground his hips against her again. She writhed against him, increasing the delicious friction against the tight bundle of nerves.

Ryan gripped the base of his cock and pressed its head to her entrance. He inched inside, and Tess whimpered softly. She dug her fingers into his hips, her eyes meeting his as he slid the rest of the way home. Until he was nestled as deeply inside her as the laws of physics would allow.

When he was fully seated, her slick, heated flesh surrounding him, an involuntary growl escaped his mouth at the delicious feel of this woman who was all softness and curves. Sweetness and beauty. His friend and his lover.

His gaze met hers as he hovered above her and moved inside her. His voice rasping, he whispered to her. Told her how incredible she made him feel.

Then, lifting her legs, he hooked them over his shoulders as he leaned over her, his weight on his hands as he moved.

She gasped, her eyes widening at the sensation of him going deep and hitting bottom due to the sudden shift in position.

"Ryan… I…oh… God." Tessa squeezed her eyes shut.

"C'mon, Tess." He arched his back as he shifted his hips forward, beads of sweat forming on his brow and trickling down his back. "Just let go. Don't think. Just feel."

Her breath came in quick pants, and she dug her nails in his biceps. Suddenly, her mouth formed a little *O* and her eyes opened wide. The unmis-

takable expression of pure satisfaction that overtook her as she called his name was one of the
most beautiful things he'd ever seen. Something
he wanted to see again and again.

Her flesh throbbed and pulsed around him,
bringing him to his peak. He tensed, shuddering as he cursed and called her name.

Ryan collapsed on to the bed beside her, both
of them breathing hard and staring at the ceiling
overhead for a few moments.

Finally, she draped an arm over his abdomen
and rested her head on his shoulder.

He kissed the top of her head, pulled the covers over them, and slipped an arm around her.
He lay there, still and quiet, fighting his natural
tendency to slip out into the night. His usual MO
after a one-night stand. Only he couldn't do that.
Partly because it was Tess. Partly because what
he'd felt between them was something he couldn't
quite name, and he wanted to feel it again.

Ryan propped an arm beneath his head and
stared at the ceiling as Tessa's soft breathing indicated she'd fallen asleep.

* * *

Intimacy.

That was the elusive word he'd been searching for all night. The thing he'd felt when his eyes had met hers as he'd roared, buried deep inside her. He'd sounded ridiculous. Like a wounded animal, in pain. Needing someone to save him.

Ryan scrubbed a hand down his face, one arm still wrapped around his best friend. Whom he'd made love to. The woman who knew him better than anyone in the world.

And now they knew each other in a way they'd never allowed themselves to before. A way that made him feel raw and exposed, like a live wire.

While making love to Tess, he'd felt a surge of power as he'd teased her gorgeous body and coaxed her over the edge. Watched her free-fall into ecstasy, her body trembling.

But as her inner walls pulsed, pulling him over the cliff after her, he'd felt something completely foreign and yet vaguely familiar. It was a thing he couldn't name. Or maybe he hadn't wanted to.

Then when he'd startled awake, his arm slightly

numb from being wedged beneath her, the answer was on his tongue.

Intimacy.

How was it that he'd managed to have gratifying sex with women without ever experiencing this heightened level of intimacy? Not even with his ex—the woman he'd planned to marry.

He and Sabrina had known each other. What the other wanted for breakfast. Each other's preferred drinks. They'd even known each other's bodies. *Well.* And yet he'd never experienced this depth of connection. Of truly being known by someone who could practically finish his sentences. Not because Tessa was so like him, but because she understood him in a way no one else did.

Ryan swallowed the hard lump clogging his throat and swiped the backs of his fingers over his damp brow.

Why is it suddenly so goddamned hot in here?

He blew out a long, slow breath. Tried to slow the rhythm of his heart, suddenly beating like a drum.

What the hell had he just done?

He'd satisfied the curiosity that had been simmering just below the surface of his friendship with Tessa. The desire to know her intimately. To know how it would feel to have her soft curves pressed against him as he'd surged inside her.

Now he knew what it was like for their bodies to move together. As if they were a single being. How it made his pulse race like a freight train as she called his name in a sweet, husky voice he'd never heard her use before. The delicious burn of her nails gently scraping his back as she wrapped her legs around him and pulled him in deeper.

And how it felt as she'd throbbed and pulsed around his heated flesh until he could no longer hold back his release.

Now, all he could think about was feeling all of those things again. Watching her shed the inhibitions that had held her back at first. Taking her a little further.

But Tessa was his best friend, and a very good friend's sister. He'd crossed the line. Broken a promise and taken them to a place they could never venture back from. After last night, he couldn't see her and not want her. Would never forget the taste and feel of her.

So what now?

Tess was sweet and sensitive. Warm and thoughtful. She deserved more than being friends with benefits. She deserved a man as kind and loving as she was.

Was he even capable of being that kind of man?

His family was nothing like the Nobles. Hank and Loretta Bateman weren't the doting parents that kissed injured knees and cheered effort. They believed in tough love, hard lessons and that failure wasn't to be tolerated by anyone with the last name Bateman.

Ryan knew unequivocally that his parents loved him, but he was twenty-nine years old and could never recall hearing either of them say the words explicitly.

He'd taken the same approach in his relationships. It was how he was built, all he'd ever known. But Tess could never be happy in a relationship like that.

Ryan sucked in another deep breath and released it quietly. He gently kissed the top of her head and screwed his eyes shut. Allowed himself to surrender to the sleep that had eluded him until now.

They'd figure it all out in the morning. After he'd gotten some much-needed sleep. He always thought better with a clear head and a full stomach.

Twelve

Tessa's eyes fluttered opened. She blinked against the rays of light peeking through the hotel room curtain and rubbed the sleep from her eyes with her fist. Her leg was entwined with Ryan's, and one of her arms was buried beneath him.

She groaned, pressing a hand to her mouth to prevent a curse from erupting from her lips. She'd made love with her best friend. Had fallen asleep with him. She peeked beneath the covers, her mouth falling open.

Naked. Both of them.

Tessa snapped her mouth shut and eased the

cover back down. Though it didn't exactly lie flat. Not with Ryan Bateman sporting a textbook definition of morning wood.

She sank her teeth into her lower lip and groaned internally. Her nipples hardened, and the space between her thighs grew incredibly wet. Heat filled her cheeks.

She'd been with Ryan in the most intimate way imaginable. And it had been…incredible. Better than anything she'd imagined. And she'd imagined it more than she cared to admit.

Ryan had been intense, passionate and completely unselfish. He seemed to get off on pleasing her. Had evoked reactions from her body she hadn't believed it capable of. And the higher he'd taken her, the more desperate she became to shatter the mask of control that gripped his handsome face.

Tessa drew her knees to her chest and took slow, deep breaths. Willed her hands to stop shaking. Tried to tap into the brain cells that had taken a siesta the moment she'd pressed her lips to Ryan's.

Yes, sex between them had been phenomenal. But the friendship they shared for more than two decades—that was something she honestly couldn't do without.

She needed some space, so she could clear her head and make better decisions than she had last night. Last night she'd allowed her stupid crush on her best friend to run wild. She'd bought into the Cinderella fantasy. Lock, stock and barrel.

What did she think would happen next? That he'd suddenly realize she was in love with him? Maybe even realize he was in love with her, too?

Not in this lifetime or the next.

She simply wasn't that lucky. Ryan had always considered her a friend. His best friend, but nothing more. A few hours together naked between the sheets wouldn't change that.

Besides, as her mother often reminded her, tigers don't change their stripes.

How many times had Ryan said it? *Sex is just sex.* A way to have a little fun and let off a little steam. Why would she expect him to feel differently just because it was her?

Her pent-up feelings for Ryan were her issue, not his.

Tessa's face burned with an intense heat, as if she was standing too close to a fire. Waking up naked with her best friend was awkward, but they could laugh it off. Blame it on the alcohol, like Jamie Foxx. Chalk it up to them both getting too carried away in the moment. But if she told him how she really felt about him, and he rejected her...

Tessa sighed. The only thing worse than secretly lusting after her best friend was having had him, knowing just how good things could be, and then being patently rejected. She'd never recover from that. Would never be able to look him in the face and pretend everything was okay.

And if, by some chance, Ryan was open to trying to turn this into something more, he'd eventually get bored with their relationship. As he had with every relationship he'd been in before. They'd risk destroying their friendship.

It wasn't worth the risk.

Tessa wiped away tears that stung the corners

of her eyes. She quietly climbed out of bed, in search of her clothing.

She cursed under her breath as she retrieved her panties—the only clothing she'd been wearing when they entered the bedroom. Tessa pulled them on and grabbed Ryan's shirt from the floor. She slipped it on and buttoned a few of the middle buttons. She glanced back at his handsome form as he slept soundly, hoping everything between them would be all right.

Tessa slowly turned the doorknob and the door creaked open.

Damn.

Wasn't oiling door hinges part of the planned maintenance for a place like this? Did they not realize the necessity of silent hinges in the event a hotel guest needed a quiet escape after making a questionable decision with her best friend the night before?

Still, as soundly as Ryan was sleeping, odds were, he hadn't heard it.

"Tess?" Ryan called from behind her in that sexy, sleep-roughened voice that made her squirm.

Every. Damn. Time.

She sucked in a deep breath, forced a nonchalant smile and turned around. "Yes?"

"Where are you going?"

He'd propped himself up in bed on one elbow as he rubbed his eyes and squinted against the light. His brown hair stood all over his head in the hottest damn case of bed head she'd ever witnessed. And his bottle-green eyes glinted in the sunlight.

Trying to escape before you woke up. Isn't it obvious?

Tessa jerked a thumb over her shoulder. "I was about to hop into the shower, and I didn't want to wake you."

"Perfect." He sat up and threw off the covers. "We can shower together." A devilish smile curled his red lips. "I know how you feel about conserving water."

"You want to shower…together? The two of us?" She pointed to herself and then to him.

"Why? Were you thinking of inviting someone else?"

"Smart-ass." Her cheeks burned with heat. Ryan was in rare form. "You know what I meant."

"Yes, I do." He stalked toward her naked, at more than half-mast now. Looking like walking, talking sex-on-a-stick promising unicorn orgasms.

Ryan looped his arms around her waist and pressed her back against the wall. He leaned down and nuzzled her neck.

Tessa's beaded nipples rubbed against his chest through the fabric of the shirt she was wearing. Her belly fluttered, and her knees trembled. Her chest rose and fell with heavy, labored breaths. As if Ryan was sucking all the oxygen from the room, making it harder for her to breathe.

"C'mon, Tess." He trailed kisses along her shoulder as he slipped the shirt from it. "Don't make this weird. It's just us."

She raised her eyes to his, her heart racing. "It's already weird *because* it's just us."

"Good point." He gave her a cocky half smile and a micro nod. "Then we definitely need to do something to alleviate the weirdness."

"And *how* exactly are we going to do—" Tess squealed as Ryan suddenly lifted her and heaved her over his shoulder. He carried her, kicking and wiggling, into the master bathroom and turned on the water.

"Ryan Bateman, don't you dare even think about it," Tessa called over her shoulder, kicking her feet and holding on to Ryan's back for dear life.

He wouldn't drop her. She had every confidence of that. Still…

"You're going to ruin my hair."

"I like your curls better. In fact, I felt a little cheated that I didn't get to run my fingers through them. I always wanted to do that."

Something about his statement stopped her objections cold. Made visions dance in her head of them together in the shower with Ryan doing just that.

"Okay. Just put me down."

Ryan smacked her bottom lightly before setting her down, her body sliding down his. Seeming to rev them both up as steam surrounded them.

She slowly undid the three buttons of Ryan's shirt and made a show of sliding the fabric down one shoulder, then the other.

His green eyes darkened. His chest rose and fell heavily as his gaze met hers again after he'd followed the garment's descent to the floor.

Ryan hooked his thumbs into the sides of her panties and tugged her closer, dropping another kiss on her neck. He gently sank his teeth into her delicate flesh, nibbling the skin there as he glided her underwear over the swell of her bottom and down her hips.

She stepped out of them and into the shower. Pressed her back against the cool tiles. A striking contrast to the warm water. Ryan stepped into the shower, too, closing the glass door behind him and covering her mouth with his.

Tessa lay on her back, her hair wound in one of Ryan's clean, cotton T-shirts. He'd washed her hair and taken great delight in running a soapy loofah over every inch of her body.

Then he'd set her on the shower bench and

dropped to his knees. He'd used the removable shower head as a makeshift sex toy. Had used it to bring her to climax twice. Then showed her just how amazing he could be with his tongue.

When he'd pressed the front of her body to the wall, lifted one of her legs, and taken her from behind, Tessa honestly hadn't thought it would be possible for her to get there again.

She was wrong.

She came hard, her body tightening and convulsing, and his did the same soon afterward.

They'd gone through their morning routines, brushing their teeth side by side, wrapped in towels from their shower together. Ryan ordered room service, and they ate breakfast in bed, catching the last half of a holiday comedy that was admittedly a pretty crappy movie overall. Still, it never failed to make the two of them laugh hysterically.

When the movie ended, Ryan had clicked off the television and kissed her. A kiss that slowly stoked the fire low in her belly all over again.

Made her nipples tingle and the space between her thighs ache for him.

She lay staring up at Ryan, his hair still damp from the shower. Clearly hell-bent on using every single condom in that strip before the morning ended, he'd sheathed himself and entered her again.

Her eyes had fluttered closed at the delicious fullness as Ryan eased inside her. His movements were slow, deliberate, controlled.

None of those words described the Ryan Bateman she knew. The man she'd been best friends with since they were both still in possession of their baby teeth.

Ryan was impatient. Tenacious. Persistent. He wanted everything five minutes ago. But the man who hovered over her now, his piercing green eyes boring into her soul and grasping her heart, was in no hurry. He seemed to relish the torturously delicious pleasure he was giving her with his slow, languid movements.

He was laser-focused. His brows furrowed, and his forehead beaded with sweat. The sudden swivel of his hips took her by surprise, and she whimpered with pleasure, her lips parting.

Ryan leaned down and pressed his mouth to hers, slipping his tongue inside and caressing her tongue.

Tessa got lost in his kiss. Let him rock them both into a sweet bliss that left her feeling like she was floating on a cloud.

She held on to him as he arched his back, his muscles straining as his own orgasm overtook him. Allowed herself to savor the warmth that encircled her sated body.

Then, gathering her to his chest, he removed her makeshift T-shirt turban and ran his fingers through her damp, curly hair.

She'd never felt more cherished or been more satisfied in her life. Yet, when the weekend ended, it would be the equivalent of the clock striking twelve for Cinderella. The dream would be over, her carriage would turn back into a pumpkin, and she'd be the same old Tessa Noble whom Ryan only considered a friend.

She inhaled his scent. Leather and cedar with

a hint of patchouli. A scent she'd bought him for Christmas three years ago. Ryan had been wearing it ever since. Tess was never sure if he wore it because he truly liked it or because he'd wanted to make her happy.

Now she wondered the same thing about what'd happened between them this weekend. He'd tailored the entire weekend to her. Had seemed determined to see to it that she felt special, pampered.

Had she been the recipient of a pity fuck?

The possibility of Ryan sleeping with her out of a sense of charity made her heart ache.

She tried not to think of what would happen when the weekend ended. To simply enjoy the moment between them here and now.

Tessa was his until "midnight." Then the magic of their weekend together would be over, and it would be time for them to return to the real world.

Thirteen

Ryan studied Tessa as she gathered her beauty products and stowed them back into her travel bag in preparation for checkout. They'd had an incredible weekend together. With the exception of the time they spent politely posing for the reporter at dinner and waxing poetic about their friendship, they'd spent most of the weekend just a few feet away in Ryan's bed.

But this morning Tessa had seemed withdrawn. Before he'd even awakened, she'd gotten out of bed, packed her luggage, laid out what she planned to wear to the football game, and showered.

Tessa opened a tube of makeup.

"You're wearing makeup to the game?" He stepped behind her in the mirror.

"Photos before the game." She gave his reflection a cursory glance. "Otherwise, I'd just keep it simple. Lip gloss, a little eye shadow. Mascara."

She went back to silently pulling items out of her makeup bag and lining them up on the counter.

"Tess, did I do something wrong? You seem really... I don't know...distant this morning."

A pained look crimped her features, and she sank her teeth into her lower lip before turning to face him. She heaved a sigh, and though she looked in his direction, she was clearly looking past him.

"Look, Rye, this weekend has been amazing. But I think it's in the best interest of our friendship if we go back to the way things were. Forget this weekend ever happened." She shifted her gaze to his. "I honestly feel that it's the only way our friendship survives this."

"Why?"

His question reeked of quiet desperation, but he could care less. The past two days had been the best days of his life. He thought they had been for her, too. So her request hit him like a sucker punch to the gut, knocking the wind out of him.

She took the shower cap off her head, releasing the long, silky hair she'd straightened with a blow-dryer attachment before they'd met Greg at the restaurant for dinner the night before.

"Because the girl you were attracted to on that stage isn't who I am. I can't maintain all of this." She indicated the makeup on the counter and her straightened hair. "It's exhausting. More importantly, it isn't me. Not really."

"You think all of this is what I'm attracted to? That I can't see…that I haven't always seen you?"

"You never kissed me before, not seriously," she added before he could mention that kiss in college. "And we certainly never…" She gestured toward the bed, as if she was unable to bring herself to say the words or look at the place where he'd laid her bare and tasted every inch of her warm brown skin.

"To be fair, you kissed me." Ryan stepped closer.

She tensed, but then lifted her chin defiantly, meeting his gaze again. The rapid rise and fall of her chest, indicated that she was taking shallow breaths. But she didn't step away from him. For which he was grateful.

"You know what I mean," she said through a frustrated little pout. "You never showed any romantic interest in me before the auction. So why are you interested now? Is it because someone else showed interest in me?"

"Why would you think that?" His voice was low and gruff. Pained.

Her accusation struck him like an openhanded slap to the face. It was something his mother had often said to him as a child. That he was only interested in his old toys when she wanted to give them to someone else.

Was that what he was doing with Tess?

"Because if I had a relationship…a life of my own, then I wouldn't be a phone call away whenever you needed me." Her voice broke slightly, and she swiped at the corners of her eyes. "Or maybe it's a competitive thing. I don't know. All I know is that you haven't made a move before now. So what changed?"

The hurt in her eyes and in the tremor of her voice felt like a jagged knife piercing his chest.

She was right. He was a selfish bastard. Too much of a coward to explore his attraction to her. Too afraid of how it might change their relationship.

"I… I…" His throat tightened, and his mouth felt dry as he sought the right words. But Tessa was his best friend, and they'd always shot straight with each other. "Sex, I could get anywhere." He forced his gaze to meet hers. Gauged her reaction. "But what we have… I don't have that with anyone else, Tess. I didn't want to take a chance on losing you. Couldn't risk screwing up our friendship like I've screwed up every relationship I've ever been in."

She dropped her gaze, absently dragging her fingers through her hair and tugging it over one shoulder. Tess was obviously processing his words. Weighing them on her internal bullshit meter.

"So why risk it now? What's changed?" She wrapped her arms around her middle. Something she did to comfort herself.

"I don't know." He whispered the words, his eyes not meeting hers.

It was a lie.

Tess was right. He'd been prompted to action by his fear of losing her. He'd been desperate to stake his claim on Tess. Wipe thoughts of any other man from her brain.

In the past, she had flirted with the occasional guy. Even dated a few. But none of them seemed to pose any real threat to what they shared. But when she'd stood on that stage as the sexiest god-damn woman in the entire room with men falling all over themselves to spend a few hours with her…suddenly everything was different. For the first time in his life, the threat of losing his best friend to someone else suddenly became very real. And he couldn't imagine his life without her in it.

Brain on autopilot, he'd gone into caveman mode. Determined to win the bid, short of putting up the whole damn ranch in order to win her.

Tessa stared at him, her pointed gaze demanding further explanation.

"It felt like the time was right. Like Fate stepped in and gave us a nudge."

"You're full of shit, Ryan Bateman." She smacked her lips and narrowed her gaze. Arms folded over her chest, she shifted to a defensive stance. "You don't believe in Fate. 'Our lives are what we make of them.' That's what you've always said."

"I'm man enough to admit when I'm wrong. Or at least open-minded enough to explore the possibility."

She turned to walk away, but he grasped her fingertips with his. A move that was more of a plea than a demand. Still, she halted and glanced over her shoulder in his direction.

"Tess, why are you so dead set against giving this a chance?"

"Because I'm afraid of losing you, too." Her voice was a guttural whisper.

He tightened his grip on her hand and tugged her closer, forcing her eyes to meet his. "You're not going to lose me, Tess. I swear, I'm not going anywhere."

"Maybe not, but we both know your MO when it comes to relationships. You rush into them, feverish and excited. But after a while you get bored, and you're ready to move on." She frowned, a pained look furrowing her brow. "What happens then, Ryan? What happens once you've pulled me in deep and then you decide you just want to go back to being friends?" She shook her head vehemently. "I honestly don't think I could handle that."

Ryan's jaw clenched. He wanted to object. Promise to never hurt her. But hadn't he hurt every woman he'd ever been with except the one woman who'd walked away from him?

It was the reason Tripp had made him promise

to leave his sister alone. Because, though they were friends, he didn't deem him good enough for his sister. Didn't trust that he wouldn't hurt her.

Tessa obviously shared Tripp's concern.

Ryan wished he could promise Tess he wouldn't break her heart. But their polar opposite approaches to relationships made it seem inevitable.

He kept his relationships casual. A means of mutual satisfaction. Because he believed in fairytale love and romance about as much as he believed in Big Foot and the Loch Ness Monster.

Tess, on the other hand, was holding out for the man who would sweep her off her feet. For a relationship like the one her parents shared. She didn't understand that Chuck and Tina Noble were the exception, rather than the rule.

Yet, despite knowing all the reasons he and Tess should walk away from this, he couldn't let her go.

Tessa's frown deepened as his silent response to her objection echoed off the walls in the elegant, tiled bathroom.

"This weekend has been amazing. You made me feel like Cinderella at the ball. But we've got the game this afternoon, then we're heading back home. The clock is about to strike midnight, and it's time for me to turn back into a pumpkin."

"You realize that you've just taken the place of the Maybach in this scenario." He couldn't help the smirk that tightened the edges of his mouth.

Some of the tension drained from his shoulders as her sensual lips quirked in a rueful smile. She shook her head and playfully punched him in the gut.

"You know what I mean. It's time for me to go back to being me. Trade my glass slippers in for a pair of Chuck Taylors."

He caught her wrist before she could walk away. Pulling her closer, he wrapped his arms around her and stared deep into those gorgeous brown eyes that had laid claim on him ever since he'd first gazed into them.

"Okay, Cinderella. If you insist that things go back to the way they were, there's not much I can do about that. But if you're mine until midnight,

I won't be cheated. Let's forget the game, stay here and make love."

"But I've already got the tickets."

"I don't care." He slowly lowered his mouth toward hers. "I'll reimburse you."

"But they're on the fifty-yard line. At the stadium that's your absolute favorite place in the world."

"Not today it isn't." He feathered a gentle kiss along the edge of her mouth, then trailed his lips down her neck.

"Ryan, we can't just blow off the—" She dug her fingers into his bare back and a low moan escaped her lips as he kissed her collarbone. The sound drifted below his waist and made him painfully hard.

"We can do anything we damn well please." He pressed a kiss to her ear. One of the many erogenous zones he'd discovered on her body during their weekend together. Tessa's knees softened, and her head lolled slightly, giving him better access to her neck.

"But the article…they're expecting us to go

to the game, and if we don't…well, everyone will think—"

"Doesn't matter what they think." He lifted her chin and studied her eyes, illuminated by the morning sunlight spilling through the windows. He dragged a thumb across her lower lip. "It only matters what you and I want."

He pressed another kiss to her lips, lingering for a moment before reluctantly pulling himself away again so he could meet her gaze. He waited for her to open her eyes again. "What do you want, Tess?"

She swallowed hard, her gaze on his lips. "I want both. To go to the game, as expected, and to spend the day in bed making love to you."

"Hmm…intriguing proposition." He kissed her again. Tess really was a woman after his own heart. "One that would require us to spend one more night here. Then we'll head back tomorrow. And if you still insist—"

"I will." There was no hesitation in her voice, only apology. She moved a hand to cradle his cheek, her gaze meeting his. "Because it's what's best for our friendship."

Ryan forced a smile and released an uneasy breath. Tried to pretend that his chest didn't feel like it was caving in. He gripped her tighter against him, lifting her as she wrapped her legs around him.

If he couldn't have her like this always, he'd take every opportunity to have her now. In the way he'd always imagined. Even if that meant they'd be a little late for the game.

Fourteen

They'd eaten breakfast, their first meal in the kitchen since they'd arrived, neither of them speaking much. The only part of their conversation that felt normal was their recap of some of the highlights during their team's win the day before. But then the conversation had returned to the stilted awkwardness they'd felt before then.

Ryan had loaded their luggage into the Maybach, and they were on the road, headed back to Royal, barely two words spoken between them before Tessa finally broke their silence.

"This is for the best, Rye. After all, you were

afraid to tell my brother about that fake kiss we had on Valentine's Day in college." Tessa grinned, her voice teasing.

Ryan practically snorted, poking out his thumb and holding it up. "A… I am *not* afraid of your brother."

Not physically, at least. Ryan was a good head taller than Tripp and easily outweighed him by twenty-five pounds of what was mostly muscle. But, in all honesty, he *was* afraid of how the weekend with Tessa would affect his friendship with Tripp. It could disrupt the connection between their families.

The Batemans and Nobles were as thick as thieves now. Had been since their fathers were young boys. But in the decades prior, the families had feuded over land boundaries, water rights and countless other ugly disputes. Some of which made Ryan ashamed of his ancestors. But everything had changed the day Tessa's grandfather had saved Ryan's father's life when he'd fallen into a well.

That fateful day, the two families had bonded.

A bond which had grown more intricate over the years, creating a delicate ecosystem he dared not disturb.

Ryan continued, adding his index finger for effect. "B… Yes, I think it might be damaging to our friendship if Tripp tries to beat my ass and I'm forced to defend myself." He added a third finger, hesitant to make his final point. An admission that made him feel more vulnerable than he was comfortable being, even with Tess. "And C…it wasn't a fake kiss. It was a little too real. Which is why I've tried hard to never repeat it."

Ryan's pulse raced, and his throat suddenly felt dry. He returned his other hand to the steering wheel and stared at the road ahead. He didn't need to turn his head to know Tessa was staring at him. The heat of her stare seared his skin and penetrated his chest.

"Are you saying that since that kiss—" Her voice was trembling, tentative.

"Since that kiss, I've recognized that the attraction between us went both ways." He rushed the words out, desperate to stop her from asking what he suspected she might.

Why hadn't he said anything all those years ago? Or in the years since that night?

He'd never allowed himself to entertain either question. Doing so was a recipe for disaster.

Why court disaster when they enjoyed an incomparable friendship? Shouldn't that be good enough?

"Oh." The disappointment in her voice stirred heaviness in his chest, rather than the ease and lightness he usually felt when they were together.

When Ryan finally glanced over at his friend, she was staring at him blankly, as if there was a question she was afraid to ask.

"Why haven't you ever said anything?"

Because he hadn't been ready to get serious about anyone back then. And Tessa Noble wasn't the kind of girl you passed the time with. She was the genuine deal. The kind of girl you took home to mama. And someone whose friendship meant everything to him.

"Bottom line? I promised your brother I'd treat

you like an honorary little sister. That I'd never lay a hand on you." A knot tightened in his belly. "A promise I've obviously broken."

"Wait, you two just decided, without consulting me? Like I'm a little child and you two are my misfit parents? What kind of caveman behavior is that?"

Ryan winced. Tessa was angry, and he didn't blame her. "To be fair, we had this conversation when he and I were about fourteen. Long before you enlightened us on the error of our anti-feminist tendencies. Still, it's a promise I've always taken seriously. Especially since, at the time, I did see you as a little sister. Obviously, things have changed since then."

"When?" Her tone was soft, but demanding. As if she needed to know.

It wasn't a conversation he wanted to have, but if they were going to have it, she deserved his complete honesty.

"I first started to feel some attraction toward you when you were around sixteen." He cleared his throat, his eyes steadily on the road. "But when I left for college I realized how deep that attraction ran. I was miserable without you that first semester in college."

"You seemed to adapt pretty quickly by sleeping your way across campus," she huffed. She turned toward the window and sighed. "I shouldn't have said that. I'm sorry. I…" She didn't finish her statement.

"Forget it." Ryan released a long, slow breath. "This is uncharted territory for us. We'll learn to deal with it. Everything'll be fine."

But even as he said the words, he couldn't convince himself of their truth.

After Ryan's revelations, the ride home was awkward and unusually quiet, even as they both tried much too hard to behave as if everything was fine.

Everything most certainly was *not* fine.

Strained and uncomfortable? *Yes*. Their forced conversation, feeble smiles and weak laughter were proof they'd both prefer to be anywhere else.

And it confirmed they'd made the right decision by not pursuing a relationship. It would only destroy their friendship in the end once Ryan had tired of her and was ready to move on to someone polished and gorgeous, like his ex.

This was all her fault. She'd kissed Ryan. Tessa clenched her hands in her lap, willing them to stop trembling.

She only hoped their relationship could survive this phase of awkwardness, so things could go back to the way they were.

Tessa's phone buzzed, and she checked her text messages.

Tripp had sent a message to say that he'd landed a meeting with a prospect that had the potential to become one of their largest customers. His flight to Iowa would leave in a few days, and she would be in charge at the Noble Spur.

She scrolled to the next text and read Bo's message reminding her that she'd agreed to attend a showing of *A Christmas Carol* with him at the town's outdoor, holiday theater.

Tessa gripped her phone and turned it over in her lap, looking over guiltily at Ryan. After what had happened between them this weekend, the thought of going out with someone else turned her stomach, but she'd already promised Bo.

And even though she and Bo were going to a movie together, it could hardly be considered a date. Half the town of Royal would be there.

Would it be so wrong for them to go on a friendly outing to the movies?

Besides, maybe seeing other people was just the thing to alleviate the awkwardness between them and prompt them to forget about the past three days.

Tessa worried her lower lip with her teeth. Deep down, she knew the truth. Things would never be the same between them.

Because she wanted Ryan now more than ever.

No matter how hard she tried, Tessa would never forget their weekend together and how he'd made her feel.

Fifteen

Gus sat in his favorite recliner and put his feet up to watch a little evening television. Reruns of some of his favorite old shows. Only he held the remote in his hand without ever actually turning the television on.

The house was quiet. Too quiet.

Alexis was in Houston on business, and her brother Justin was staying in Dallas overnight with a friend.

Normally, he appreciated the solitude. Enjoyed being able to watch whatever the hell he wanted on television without one of the kids scoffing about him watching an old black-and-white movie or an episode of one of his favorite shows that he'd seen half a dozen times before. But lately, it had been harder to cheerfully bear his solitude.

During the months he and Rose had worked together to split up Daniel and Alexis, he'd found himself enjoying her company. So much so that he preferred it mightily to being alone in this big old house.

Gus put down the remote and paced the floor. He hadn't seen Rose since the night of the bachelor auction at the Texas Cattleman's Club. They'd spoken by phone twice, but just to confirm that their plan had worked.

As far as they could tell, Alexis and Daniel were no longer seeing each other. And both of them seemed to be in complete misery.

Gus had done everything he could to try and cheer Alexis up. But the pain in her eyes persisted. As did the evidence that she'd still been crying from time to time.

He'd tried to get his granddaughter to talk about it, but she'd insisted that it wasn't anything she couldn't handle. And she said he wouldn't understand anyway.

That probably hurt the most. Especially since he really did understand how she was feeling. And worse, he and Rose had been the root cause of that pain.

The guilt gnawed at his gut and broke his heart.

Rose had reminded him of why they'd first hatched the plan to break up Daniel and Alexis. Their families had been mortal enemies for decades. Gus and Rose had hated each other so much they were willing to work together in order to prevent their grandchildren from being involved with each other. Only, Gus hadn't reckoned on coming to enjoy the time he spent with Rose Clayton. And he most surely hadn't anticipated that he'd find himself getting sweet on her again after all these years.

He was still angry at Rose for how she'd treated him all those years ago, when he'd been so very in love with her. But now he understood that because of her cruel father, holding the welfare of her ill mother over Rose's head, she'd felt she had no choice but to break it off with him and marry someone Jedediah Clayton had deemed worthy.

He regretted not recognizing the distress Rose was in back then. That her actions had been a cry for help. Signs he and his late wife, Sarah, who had once been Rose's best friend, had missed.

Gus heaved a sigh and glanced over his shoulder at the television. His reruns could wait.

Gus left the Lone Wolf Ranch and headed over to Rose's place, The Silver C, one last time to say goodbye. Maybe share a toast to the success of their plan to look out for Alexis and Daniel in the long run, even if the separation was hurting them both now.

The property had once been much vaster than his. But over the years, he'd bought quite a bit of it. Rose had begrudgingly sold it to him in order to pay off the gambling debts of her late husband, Ed.

Rose's father must be rolling over in his grave because the ranch hand he'd judged unworthy of his daughter was now in possession of much of the precious land the man had sought to keep out of his hands. Gus didn't normally think ill of the dead. But in Jedediah's case, he was willing to make an exception.

When Gus arrived at The Silver C, all decked out in its holiday finest, Rose seemed as thrilled to see him as he was to see her.

"Gus, what on earth are you doing here?" A smile lighting her eyes, she pulled the pretty red sweater she was wearing around her more tightly as cold air rushed in from outside.

"After all these months working together, I thought it was only right that we had a proper goodbye." He held up a bottle of his favorite top-shelf whiskey.

Rose laughed, a joyful sound he still had fond memories of. "Well, by all means, come on in."

She stepped aside and let Gus inside. The place smelled of pine from the two fresh Christmas trees Rose had put up. One in the entry hall and another in the formal living room. And there was the unmistakable scent of fresh apple pie.

Rose directed Gus to have a seat on the sofa in the den where she'd been watching television.

Then she brought two glasses and two slices of warm apple pie on a little silver tray.

"That homemade pie?" Gus inquired as she set the tray on the table.

"Wouldn't have it any other way." She grinned, handing him a slice and a fork. She opened the bottle of whiskey and poured each of them a glass, neat.

She sat beside him and watched him with interest as he took his first bite of pie.

"Hmm, hmm, hmm. Now that's a little slice of heaven right there." He grinned.

"I'm glad you like it. And since we're celebrating our successful plot to save the kids from a disastrous future, pie seems fitting." She smiled, but it seemed hollow. She took a sip of the whiskey and sighed. "Smooth."

"That's one of the reasons I like it so much." He nodded, shoveling another bite of pie into his mouth and chewing thoughtfully. He surveyed the space and leaned closer, lowering his voice. "Daniel around today?"

"No, he's gone to Austin to handle some ranch

business." She raised an eyebrow, her head tilted. "Why?"

"No reason in particular." Gus shrugged, putting down his pie plate and sipping his whiskey. "Just wanted to ask how the boy is doing. He still as miserable as my Alexis?"

Pain and sadness were etched in Rose's face as she lowered her gaze and nodded. "I'm afraid so. He's trying not to show how hurt he is, but I honestly don't think I've ever seen him like this. He's already been through so much with his mother." She sighed, taking another sip of whiskey. Her hands were trembling slightly as she shook her head. "I hope we've done the right thing here. I guess I didn't realize how much they meant to each other." She sniffled and pulled a tissue out of her pocket, dabbing at her eyes.

Rose forced a laugh. "I'm sorry. You must think me so ridiculous sitting here all teary-eyed over having gotten the very thing we both wanted."

Gus put down his glass and took Rose's hand between his. It was delicate and much smaller than his own. Yet, they were the hands of a woman who had worked a ranch her entire life.

"I understand just what you're feeling." He stroked her wrist with his thumb. "Been feeling pretty guilty, too. And second-guessing our decision."

"Oh, Gus, we spent so many years heartbroken and angry. It changed us, and not for the better." Tears leaked from Rose's eyes, and her voice broke. "I just hope we haven't doomed Alexis and Daniel to the same pain and bitterness."

"It's going to be okay, Rose." He took her in his arms and hugged her to his chest. Tucked her head beneath his chin as he swayed slowly and stroked her hair. "We won't allow that to happen to Alexis and Daniel. I promise."

"God, I hope you're right. They deserve so much more than that. Both of them." She held on to him. One arm wrapped around him and the other was pressed to his chest.

He should be focused on Daniel and Alexis and the dilemma that he and Rose had created. Gus realized that. Yet, an awareness of Rose slowly spread throughout his body. Sparks of electricity danced along his spine.

He rubbed her back and laid a kiss atop her head. All of the feelings he'd once experienced when he'd held Rose in his arms as a wet-behind-the-ears ranch hand came flooding back to him. Overwhelmed his senses, making his heart race in a way he'd forgotten that it could.

After all these years, he still had a thing for Rose Clayton. Still wanted her.

Neither of them had moved or spoken for a while. They just held each other in silence, enjoying each other's comfort and warmth.

Finally, Rose pulled away a little and tipped her head, her gaze meeting his. She leaned in closer, her mouth hovering just below his, her eyes drifting closed.

Gus closed the space between them, his lips meeting hers in a kiss that was soft and sweet. Almost chaste.

He slipped his hands on either side of her face, angling it to give him better access to her mouth. Ran his tongue along her lips that tasted of smooth whiskey and homemade apple pie.

Rose sighed with satisfaction, parting her lips. She clutched at his shirt, pulling him as close as their position on the sofa would allow.

She murmured with pleasure when he slipped his tongue between her lips.

Time seemed to slow as they sat there, their mouths seeking each other's out in a kiss that grew hotter. Greedier. More intense.

There was a fire in his belly that he hadn't felt in ages. One that made him want things with Rose he hadn't wanted in so long.

Gus forced himself to pull away from Rose. He gripped her shoulders, his eyes searching hers for permission.

Rose stood up. She switched off the television with the remote, picked up their two empty whiskey glasses, then walked toward the stairs that led to the upper floor of The Silver C. Looking back at him, she flashed a wicked smile that did things to him.

"Are you coming or not?"

Gus nearly knocked over the silver tray on the table in front of him in his desperation to climb to his feet. He hurried toward her but was halted by her next words.

"Don't forget the bottle."

"Yes, ma'am." Grinning, he snatched it off the table before grabbing her hand and following her up the stairs.

Sixteen

When he heard his name called, Ryan looked up from where Andy, his farrier, was shoeing one of the horses.

It was Tripp.

The muscles in Ryan's back tensed. He hadn't talked to Tess or Tripp in the three days since they'd been back from their trip to Dallas. He could tell by his friend's expression that Tripp was concerned about something.

Maybe he had come to deliver a much-deserved ass-whipping. After all, Ryan had broken his promise by sleeping with Tess.

"What's up, Tripp?" Ryan walked over to his friend, still gauging the man's mood.

"I'm headed to the airport shortly, but I need to ask a favor."

"Sure. Anything."

"Keep an eye on Tess, will you?"

Ryan hadn't expected that. "Why, is something wrong?"

"Not exactly." Tripp removed his Stetson and adjusted it before placing it back on his head. "It's just that Mom and Dad are still gone, and I'm staying in Des Moines overnight. She'll be kicking around that big old house by herself mostly. We let a few hands off for the holidays. Plus... I don't like that Bo and Clem have been sniffing around the last few days. I'm beginning to think that letting Tessa participate in that bachelor auction was a mistake."

Ryan tugged his baseball cap down on his head, unsettled by the news of Bo and Clem coming around. He'd paid a hefty sum at the auction to ward those two off. Apparently, they hadn't gotten the hint.

"First, if you think you *let* your sister participate in that bachelor's auction, you don't know your sister very well. Tess has got a mind of her own. Always has. Always will."

"Guess you're right about that." Tripp rubbed the back of his neck. "And I'm not saying that Bo or Clem are bad guys. They're nice enough, I guess."

"Just not when they come calling on your sister." Ryan chuckled. He knew exactly how Tripp felt.

"Yeah, pretty much."

"Got a feeling the man you'll think is good enough for your little sister ain't been born yet."

"And probably never will be." Tripp chuckled. "But as her big brother, it's my job to give any guy who comes around a hard time. Make him prove he's worthy."

"Well, just hold your horses there, buddy. It's not like she's considering either of them." Ryan tried to appear nonchalant about the whole ordeal. Though on the inside he felt like David Banner in the midst of turning into the Incredible Hulk.

He wanted to smash both Bo and Clem upside the head and tell them to go sniffing around someone else. "I think you're getting a little ahead of yourself."

"You haven't been around since you guys got back." The statement almost sounded accusatory. "Looks like the flower show threw up in our entry hall."

"Clem and Bo have been sending Tessa flowers?" Ryan tried to keep his tone and his facial expression neutral. He counted backward from ten in his head.

"Clem's apparently determined to empty out the local florist. Bo, on the other hand, has taken Tessa out to some play and this afternoon they're out riding."

Ryan hoped like hell that Tripp didn't notice the tick in his jaw or the way his fists clenched at his sides.

Tripp flipped his wrist, checking his watch. "Look, I'd better get going. I'll be back tomorrow afternoon, but call me if you need anything."

"Will do." Ryan tipped the brim of his baseball hat. "Safe travels."

He watched his friend climb back into his truck and head toward the airport in Dallas.

Jaw clenched, Ryan uncurled his fists and reminded himself to calm down. Then he saddled up Phantom, his black quarter horse stallion, and went for a ride.

For the past few days, he hadn't been able to stop thinking about his weekend with Tess. The moments they'd shared replayed again and again in his head. Distracted him from his work. Kept him up staring at the ceiling in the middle of the night.

He knew Tess well. Knew she'd been as affected by their weekend together as he had. So how could she dismiss what they'd shared so easily and go out with Bo, or for God's sake, Clem?

Phantom's hooves thundered underneath him as the cold, brisk air slapped him in the face. He'd hoped that his ride would calm him down and help him arrive at the same conclusion Tess had. That it would be better for everyone if they remained friends.

But no matter how hard and fast he'd ridden, it didn't drive away his desire for Tess. Nor did it ease the fury that rose in his chest at the thought of another man touching her the way he had. The way he wanted to again.

He recognized the validity of Tessa's concerns that he wasn't serious and that he'd be chasing after some other skirt in a few months. He couldn't blame her for feeling that way. After all, as Helene was fond of saying, the proof was in the pudding.

He wouldn't apologize for his past. Because he'd never lied to or misled any of the women he'd dated. So he certainly wouldn't give his best friend any sense of false hope that he'd suddenly convert to the romantic suitor he'd been over the course of the weekend, for the sake of the Texas Cattleman's Club.

Ryan wasn't that guy any more than Tessa was the kind of woman who preferred a pair of expensive, red-bottomed heels to a hot new pair of sneakers.

So why couldn't he let go of the idea of the two of them being together?

He'd asked himself that question over and over the past few days, and the same answer kept rising above all the bullshit excuses he'd manufactured.

He craved the intimacy that they shared.

It was the thing that made his heart swell every time he thought of their weekend together. The thing that made it about so much more than just the sex.

He'd even enjoyed planning their weekend. And he'd derived a warm sense of satisfaction from seeing her reaction to each of his little surprises.

Ryan had always believed that people who made a big show of their relationships were desperate to make other people believe they were happy. But despite his romantic gestures being part of a ruse to keep the club from being mired in scandal, they had brought him and Tess closer. Shown her just how much he valued her.

Maybe he didn't believe that love was rainbows and sugarplums. Or that another person was the key to his happiness. But he knew unquestionably that he would be miserable if Tess got involved with someone else.

He couldn't promise her that he'd suddenly sweep her off her feet like some counterfeit Prince Charming. But he sure as hell wanted to try, before she walked into the arms of someone else.

Ryan and Phantom returned to the stables, and he handed him off to Andy. Then he hurried into the house to take a shower. He needed to see Tess right away.

Seventeen

Tessa checked her phone. The only messages were from Tripp, letting her know that his plane had landed safely, and from Clem asking if she'd received his flowers ahead of their casual dinner date later that night.

She tossed the phone on the counter. No messages from Ryan. They'd maintained radio silence since he'd set her luggage in the entry hall, said goodbye, and driven off.

Tessa realized that the blame wasn't all his. After all, the phone worked both ways. On a typical day, she would've called her best friend a couple of times by now. She was clearly avoiding him, as much as he was avoiding her.

She was still angry that Ryan and Tripp had made a pact about her. As if she were incapable of making her own decisions. Mostly, she was hurt that Ryan hadn't countered her accusation that he'd eventually tire of her and move on to someone else.

She wanted him to deny it. To fight for her. But Ryan hadn't raised the slightest objection. Which meant what he really wanted was a no-strings fuck buddy until something better came along.

For her, that would never be enough with Ryan. She was already in way too deep. But the truth was, she would probably never be enough for him. She was nothing like the lithe, glamorous women who usually caught Ryan's eye. Women like Sabrina Calhoun who was probably born wearing a pair of Louboutins and carrying an Hermès bag. Or women like Lana, the overly friendly barmaid. Women who exuded sex and femininity rather than looking like they shopped at Ranchers R Us.

Headlights shone in the kitchen window. Someone was in the driveway. As soon as the vehicle pulled up far enough, Tess could see it clearly.

It was Ryan's truck.

Her belly fluttered, and her muscles tensed. She waited for him to come to the kitchen door, but he didn't. Instead, he made a beeline for the stables.

Ryan had likely come to check on the stables at Tripp's request. He was obviously still avoiding her, and she was over it.

Nervousness coiled through her and knotted in her belly. They both needed to be mature about this whole thing. Starting right now.

She wouldn't allow the fissure between them to crack open any wider. If that meant she had to be the one to break the ice, she would.

Tessa's hair, piled on top of her head in a curly bun, was still damp from the shower. She'd thrown on an old graphic T-shirt and a pair of jeans, so she could run out and double-check the stables.

Not her best look.

Tess slipped on a jacket and her boots and trudged out to the stables.

"Hey." She approached him quietly, her arms folded across her body.

"Hey." Ryan leaned against the wall. "Sorry, I haven't called. Been playing catch-up since we returned."

"I've been busy, too." She pulled the jacket tighter around her.

"I heard. Word is you've got a date tonight." The resentment in his voice was unmistakable. "You spent the weekend in my bed. A few days later and suddenly you and Bo are a thing and Clem is sending you a houseful of flowers?"

"Bo and I aren't *a thing*. We've just gone out a couple times. As friends." Her cheeks were hot. "And despite what happened this weekend, you and I *aren't* a thing. So you don't get a say in who I do or don't spend time with." The pitch of her voice was high, and the words were spilling out of her mouth. Tessa sucked in a deep breath, then continued. "Besides, are you going to tell me you've never done the same?"

Crimson spread across his cheeks. He stuffed his hands in his pockets. "That was different."

"Why? Because you're a guy?"

"Because it was casual, and neither of us had expectations for anything more."

"How is that different from what happened between us?"

Ryan was playing mind games with her, and she didn't appreciate it.

"Because I *do* expect more. That is, I want more. With you." He crept closer.

Tessa hadn't expected that. She shifted her weight from one foot to the other, her heart beating faster. "What are you saying?"

"I'm saying I want more of what we had this past weekend. That I want it to be me and you. No one else. And I'm willing to do whatever you need in order to make it happen."

"Whatever *I* need?" The joy that had been building in her chest suddenly slammed into a brick wall. "As in, you'd be doing it strictly for my benefit, not because it's what you want?"

"You make it sound as if I'm wrong for wanting you to be happy." His brows furrowed, and his mouth twisted in confusion. "How does that make me the bad guy?"

"It doesn't make you a bad person, Ryan. But I'm not looking for a fuck buddy. Not even one who happens to be my best friend." She pressed a hand to her forehead and sighed.

"I wouldn't refer to it that way, but if it makes us happy, why not?" Ryan's voice was low, his gaze sincere. He took her hand in his. "Who cares what anyone else thinks as long as it's what we want?"

"But it isn't what *I* want." Tears stung Tessa's eyes, and her voice wavered.

Ryan lifted her chin, his green eyes pinning her in place. "What *do* you want, Tess?"

"I want the entire package, Ryan. Marriage. Kids, eventually." She pulled away, her back turned to him for a moment before turning to face him again. "And I'll never get any of that if I settle for being friends with benefits."

"How can you be so sure it wouldn't work between us?" he demanded.

"Because you can't even be honest about what you want in bed with me." She huffed, her hands shaking.

There, she'd said it.

"What the hell are you talking about, Tess?"

Her face and chest were suddenly hot, and the vast barn seemed too small a space for the two of them. She slipped off her jacket and hung it on a hook.

Though the remaining ranch staff had left for the day and Tripp was gone, she still lowered her voice. As if the horses would spread gossip to the folks in town.

"I know you like it…rough. You weren't like that with me."

"Really? You're complaining about my performance?" He folded his arms, his jaw clenched.

"No, of course not. It was amazing. *You* were amazing. But I overheard Sabrina talking to a friend of hers on the phone when you two were still together. She was saying that she liked rough sex, and there was no one better at it than you."

Tessa's heart thumped. Her pulse, thundering in her ears, seemed to echo throughout the space.

"You overheard her say that on the phone?"

Tessa nodded.

"You know that wasn't an accident, right? She got a kick out of rattling your cage."

Tess suspected as much. Sabrina had never much liked her.

"You didn't answer my question." She looked in his direction, but her eyes didn't quite meet his. "No judgment. I just want to know if it's true."

"Sometimes." He shrugged. "Depends on my mood, who I'm with. And we're not talking whips and chains, if that's what you're imagining." He was clearly uncomfortable having this discussion with her. Not that she was finding it to be a walk in the park either. "Why does it matter?"

"Because if that's what you like, but with me you were…"

"Not rough," he offered tersely. "And you're angry about that?"

"Not angry. Just realistic. If you can't be yourself with me in bed, you're not going to be happy. You'll get bored and you'll want out."

Ryan stared down at her, stepping closer. "I responded to you. Gave you what I thought you wanted."

"And you did." She took a step backward, her back hitting the wall. She swallowed hard. "But did it ever occur to you that I would've liked the chance to do the same for you?"

Sighing heavily, Ryan placed one hand on the wall behind her and cradled her cheek with the other. "It's not like that's the only way I like it, Tess. I don't regret anything about my weekend with you."

"But the point was you felt you *couldn't*. Because of our friendship or maybe because of your promise to Tripp. I don't know. All I know for sure is that pretending that everything will be okay is a fool's game." She forced herself to stand taller. Chin tipped, she met his gaze.

"So that's it? Just like that, you decide that's reason enough for us to not be together?" His face was red, and anger vibrated beneath his words, though his expression remained placid.

"Isn't that reason enough for you?"

"Sex isn't everything, Tess."

"For you, it always has been. Sex is just sex, right? It's not about love or a deeper connection." The knot in Tessa's stomach tightened when Ryan dropped his gaze and didn't respond. She sighed. "Tigers can't change their stripes, Ryan. No matter how hard they might try."

She turned to dip under his arm, but he lowered it, blocking her escape from the heated look in his eyes. His closeness. His scent. Leather. Cedar. Patchouli.

Damn that patchouli.

"Ryan, what else is there for us to say?"

"Nothing." He lowered his hands to her waist and stepped closer, his body pinning hers to the wall.

Time seemed to move in slow motion as Ryan dipped his head, his lips hovering just above hers. His gaze bored into hers. She didn't dare move an inch. Didn't dare blink.

When she didn't object, his lips crushed hers in a bruising, hungry kiss that made her heart race. He tasted of Helene's famous Irish stew—one of Ryan's favorite meals—and an Irish ale.

His hands were on her hips, pinning her in place against the wall behind her. Not with enough force to hurt her, but he'd asserted himself in such a way that it was crystal clear that he wanted her there, and that she shouldn't move.

She had no plans to.

As much as she'd enjoyed seeing a gentler side of Ryan during their weekend together, the commanding look in his eye and the assertiveness of his tone revved her up in a way she would never have imagined.

He trailed his hands up her sides so damned slowly she was sure she could count the milliseconds that passed. The backs of his hands grazed her hips, her waist, the undersides of her breasts.

The apex of her thighs pulsed and throbbed with such power she felt like he might bring her over the edge just from his kiss and his demanding touch.

Her knees quivered, and her breaths were quick and shallow. His kisses grew harder, hungrier as he placed his large hands around her throat. Not squeezing or applying pressure of any real measure. But conveying a heightened sense of control.

Ryan pulled back, his body still pinning hers, but his kiss gone. After a few seconds, her eyes shot open. He was staring at her with an intensity that she might have found scary in any other situation. But she knew Ryan. Knew that he'd never do anything to hurt her.

"You still with me, Tess?"

She couldn't pry her lips open to speak, so she did the only thing she could. Her impression of a bobblehead doll.

His eyes glinted, and he smirked. Ryan leaned in and sucked her bottom lip. Gently sank his teeth into it. Then he pushed his tongue between her lips and swept it inside the cavern of her mouth. Tipped her head back so that he could deepen the kiss. Claimed her mouth as if he owned every single inch of her body and could do with it as he pleased.

Her pebbled nipples throbbed in response, and she made a small gasp as his hard chest grazed the painfully hard peaks.

His scorching, spine-tingling kiss coaxed her body into doing his bidding, and his strong hands felt as if they were everywhere at once.

Tessa sucked in a deep breath when Ryan squeezed her bottom hard, ramping up the steady throb between her thighs.

When she'd gasped, he sucked her tongue into his mouth. He lifted her higher on the wall, pinning her there with his body as he settled between her thighs.

She whimpered as his rock-hard shaft pressed against the junction of her thighs. He seemed to enjoy eliciting her soft moans as she strained her hips forward, desperate for more of the delicious friction that made her belly flutter and sent a shudder up her spine.

"Shirt and bra off," he muttered against her lips, giving her barely enough room to comply with his urgent request. But she managed eagerly enough and dropped the garments to the floor.

He lifted her higher against the wall until her breasts were level with his lips. She locked her legs around his waist, anchoring herself to the wall.

Ryan took one heavy mound in his large hand. Squeezed it, then savagely sucked at her beaded tip, upping the pain/pleasure quotient. He gently grazed the pebbled tip with his teeth, then swirled his tongue around the flesh, soothing it.

Then he moved to the other breast and did the same. This time his green eyes were locked with hers. Gauging her reaction. A wicked grin curved the edge of his mouth as he tugged her down, so her lips crashed against his again.

Could he feel the pooling between her thighs through her soaked underwear and jeans? Her cheeks heated, momentarily, at the possibility. But her embarrassment was quickly forgotten as he nuzzled her ear and whispered his next command.

"When I set you down again I want you out of every single stitch of clothing you're wearing."

"Out here? In the stable? Where anyone could see us?" she stuttered, her heart thudding wildly in her chest.

"There's no one but us here," he said matter-of-factly. "But if you want me to stop…"

"No, don't." Tess was shocked by how quickly she'd objected to ending this little game. The equivalent of begging for more of him. For more of this.

At least he hadn't made her undress alone. Ryan tugged the beige plaid shirt over his head and on to the floor, giving her a prize view of his hard abdomen. She wanted to run the tip of her tongue along the chiseled lines that outlined the rippled muscles he'd earned by working as hard on the ranch as any of his hands. To kiss and suck her way along the deep V at his hips that disappeared below his waist. Trace the ridge on the underside of his shaft with her tongue.

Ryan toed off his work boots, unzipped his jeans and shoved them and his boxers down his muscular thighs, stepping out of them.

Tess bit into her lower lip, unable to tear her

gaze from the gentle bob of his shaft as he stalked toward her and lifted her on to the edge of the adjustable, standing desk where she sometimes worked.

He raised the desk, which was in a seated position, until it was at just the right height.

"I knew this table would come in handy one day." She laughed nervously, her hands trembling slightly.

He didn't laugh, didn't smile. "Is this why you came out here, Tess? Why you couldn't be patient and wait until I came to your door?"

Before she could respond, he slid into her and they both groaned at the delicious sensation of him filling her. His back stiffened and he trembled slightly, his eyes squeezed shut.

Then he cursed under his breath and pulled out, retrieving a folded strip of foil packets from the back pocket of his jeans.

They'd both lost control momentarily. Given into the heat raging between them. But he'd come prepared. Maybe he hadn't expected to take her here in the stable or that he'd do so with such ferocity. But he had expected that at some point he'd be inside of her.

And she'd caved. Fallen under the hypnotic spell of those green eyes which negated every objection she'd posed up till then.

Sheathed now, Ryan slid inside her, his jaw tensed. He started to move slowly, but then he pulled out again.

"On your knees," he growled, before she could object.

Tessa shifted onto all fours, despite her self-consciousness about the view from behind as she arched her back and widened her stance, at his request.

Ryan adjusted the table again until it was at the perfect height. He grabbed his jeans and folded them, putting them under her knees to provide cushion.

Then suddenly he slammed into her, the sound of his skin slapping against hers filling the big, empty space. He pulled back slowly and rammed into her again. Then he slowly built a rhythm of rough and gentle strokes. Each time the head of his erection met the perfect spot deep inside her she whimpered at the pleasure building.

When he'd eased up on his movement, stopping just short of that spot, she'd slammed her hips back against him, desperate for the pleasure that the impact delivered.

Ryan reached up and slipped the tie from her hair, releasing the damp ringlets so that they fell to her shoulders and formed a curtain around her face.

He gathered her hair, winding it around his fist and tugging gently as he moved inside her. His rhythm was controlled and deliberate, even as his momentum slowly accelerated.

Suddenly, she was on her back again. Ryan had pulled out, leaned forward, and adjusted the table as high as it would go.

"Tell me what you want, Tess," he growled, his gaze locked with hers and his eyes glinted.

"I... I..." She couldn't fix her mouth to say the words, especially here under the harsh, bright lights in the stable. She averted her gaze from his.

He leaned in closer. His nostrils flared and

a subtle smirk barely turned one corner of his mouth. "Would it help if I told you I already know *exactly* what you want. I just need to hear you say it. For you to beg for it."

His eyes didn't leave hers.

"I want…" Tessa swallowed hard, her entire body trembling slightly. "Your tongue."

He leaned in closer, the smirk deepening. "Where?"

God, he was really going to make her say it.

"Here." She spread her thighs and guided his free hand between her legs, shuddering at his touch. Tess hoped that show-and-tell would do, because she was teetering on the edge, nearly ready to explode. "Please."

"That wasn't so hard, now, was it?" He leaned down and lapped at her slick flesh with his tongue.

She quivered from the pleasure that rippled through her with each stroke. He gripped her hips, holding her in place to keep her bottom at the edge of the table, so she couldn't squirm away. Despite the pleasure building to a crescendo.

Tess slid her fingers in his hair and tugged

him closer. Wanting more, even as she felt she couldn't possibly take another lash of his tongue against her sensitive flesh.

Ryan sucked on the little bundle of nerves and her body stiffened. She cursed and called his name, her inner walls pulsing.

Trailing kisses up her body, he kissed her neck. Then he guided her to her feet and turned her around, so her hands were pressed to the table and her bottom was nestled against his length.

He made another adjustment of the table, then lifted one of her knees on to it. He pressed her back down so her chest was against the table and her bottom was propped in the air.

He slid inside her with a groan of satisfaction, his hips moving against hers until finally he'd reached his own explosive release. As he gathered his breath, each pant whispered against her skin.

"Tess, I didn't mean to…" He sighed heavily. "Are you all right?"

She gave him a shaky nod, glancing back at him over her shoulder. "I'm fine."

He heaved a long sigh and placed a tender kiss on her shoulder. "Don't give up on this so easily, Tess. Or do something we'll both regret."

Ryan excused himself to find a trash can where he could discreetly discard the condom.

Tessa still hadn't moved. Her limbs quivered, and her heart raced. Slowly, she gathered her bra, her jeans and her underwear. Her legs wobbled, as if she were slightly dazed.

She put on the clothing she'd managed to gather, despite her trembling hands.

When he returned, Ryan stooped to pick up her discarded shirt. Glaring, he handed it to her.

She muttered her thanks, slipping the shirt on. "You're upset. Why? Because I brought up your sex life with Sabrina?"

"Maybe it never occurred to you that the reason Sabrina and I tended to have rough, angry sex is because we spent so much of our relationship pissed off with each other.

He put his own shirt on and buttoned it, still staring her down.

Tessa felt about two inches tall. "I hadn't considered that."

She retrieved the hair tie from the standing desk, that she'd never be able to look at again without blushing. She pulled her hair into a low ponytail, stepped into her boots, and slipped her jacket back on.

"It can be fun. Maybe even adventurous. But in the moments when you're not actually having sex, it makes for a pretty fucked-up relationship. That's not what I want for you, Tess. For us." He shook his head, his jaw still clenched. "And there's something else you failed to take into account."

"What?"

"Rough sex is what got Sabrina off. It was her thing, not mine. What gets me off is getting you there. But I guess you were too busy making your little comparisons to notice." He stalked away, then turned back, pointing a finger at her for emphasis. "I want something more with you, Tess, because we're good together. We always have been. The sex is only a small component of what makes us fit so well together. I would think that our twenty plus years of friendship should be evidence enough of that."

Tessa wished she could take back everything she'd said. That she could turn back time and get a do-over.

"Rye, I'm sorry. I didn't mean to—"

"If you don't want to be with me, Tess, that's fine. But just be honest about it. Don't make up a bunch of bullshit excuses." He tucked his plaid shirt into his well-worn jeans, then pulled on his boots before heading toward the door. "Enjoy your date with Clem."

"It's not a date," she yelled after him, her eyes stinging with tears.

He didn't respond. Just left her standing there shaking. Feeling like a fool.

And she deserved it. Every angry stare. Every word uttered in resentment.

She'd been inventing reasons for them not to be together. Because she was terrified of the truth. That she wanted to be with Ryan more than anything. She honestly did want it all—marriage, a house of her own, kids. And she wanted them with her best friend. But she wouldn't settle for being in a relationship where she was the only one in love.

And she was in love with Ryan.

But as much as she loved him, she was terrified of the deafening silence she'd face if she confessed the truth to him. Because Ryan didn't believe in messy, emotional commitments.

He'd never admitted to being in love with a single one of his girlfriends. In fact, he'd never even said that he loved Sabrina. Just that there was a spark with her that kept things exciting between them. Something he hadn't felt with anyone else.

Tessa's sight blurred with tears and she sniffled, angrily swiping a finger beneath each eye. She'd done this, and she could fix it. Because she needed Ryan in her life. And he needed her, too. Even if all they'd ever be was friends.

Tessa's phone buzzed. She pulled it from her pocket.

Clem.

She squeezed her eyes shut, her jaw clenched.

Tess hated to bail on him, but after what had happened between her and Ryan, the thought of going out with someone else made her physically ill.

She answered the phone, her fingers pressed to her throbbing temple.

"Hey, Clem, I was just about to call you. Suddenly, I'm not feeling very well."

Eighteen

Ryan hopped into his truck and pulled out of the Noble Spur like a bat out of hell. He was furious with Tess and even madder that he'd been so turned on by her when she was being completely unreasonable.

He pulled into the drive of the Bateman Ranch and parked beside an unfamiliar car. A shiny red BMW.

As Ryan approached the big house, Helene hurried to the door to meet him. By the way she was wringing that dish towel in her hand, he wasn't going to like what she had to say one bit.

He glanced at the car again, studying the license plate. Texas plates, but it could be a rental car. And only one person he knew would insist on renting a red BMW.

Hell.

This was the last thing he needed.

"Ryan, I am so sorry. I told her that you weren't home, but she insisted on waiting for you. No matter how long you were gone." She folded her arms, frowning.

"It's okay, Helene." Ryan patted the woman's shoulder and forced a smile.

"Well, well, well. Look who finally decided to come home." His ex-fiancée, Sabrina Calhoun, sashayed to the front door. "Surprised to see me, baby?"

The expression on Helene's face let him know she was fit to be tied. Never a fan of the woman, his house manager would probably sooner quit than be forced to deal with his ex's condescending attitude again.

Ryan gave Helene a low hand signal, begging

her to be civil and assuring her that everything would be all right.

Sabrina was the kind of mistake he wouldn't make twice. No matter how slick and polished she looked. Outrageously expensive clothes and purse. A haircut that cost more than most folks around here made in a week. A heavy French perfume that costed a small mint.

His former fiancée could be the dictionary illustration for high maintenance. He groaned internally, still kicking himself for ever thinking the two of them could make a life together.

Sabrina wasn't a villain. They just weren't right for each other. A reality that became apparent once she'd moved to Texas and they'd actually lived together.

Suddenly, her cute little quirks weren't so cute anymore.

"What brings you to Royal, Sabrina?" Ryan folded his arms and reared back on his heels. He asked the question as politely as he could manage.

"I happened to be in Dallas visiting a friend,

and I thought it would be rude not to come by and at least say hello." She slid her expensive sunglasses from her face and batted her eyelashes. "You think we can chat for a minute? Alone?"

She glanced briefly at Helene who looked as if she was ready to claw the woman's face off.

"Do you mind, Helene?" He squeezed her arm and gave her the same smile he'd been using to charm her out of an extra slice of pie since he was a kid.

She turned and hurried back into the house, her path littered with a string of not-so-complimentary Greek terms for Sabrina.

Ryan extended an arm toward the front door and followed Sabrina inside.

Whatever she was here for, it was better that he just let her get it out, so she could be on her merry way.

They sat down in the living room, a formal space she was well aware that his family rarely used. An indication that he didn't expect her visit to last long. And that he didn't consider her visit to be a friendly one.

"The place looks great." Sabrina glanced around.

He crossed his ankle over his knee and waited a beat before responding. "I don't mean to be rude, Brie, but we both know you're not the kind of person who'd drop by unannounced without a specific purpose in mind. I'm pressed for time today. So, it'd be great if we could just skip to the part where you ask whatever it is you came to ask."

"You know me well. Probably better than anyone." Sabrina moved from the sofa where she was seated to the opposite end of the sofa where he was situated.

Ryan watched her movement with the same suspicion with which he'd regard a rattlesnake sidling up to him. Turning slightly in his seat, so that he was facing her, he pressed a finger to his temple and waited.

He knew from experience that his silence would drive Sabrina nuts. She'd spill her guts just to fill the empty void.

"I have a little confession to make. I visited my

friend in Dallas because she emailed that article about you."

He'd nearly forgotten about that article on the bachelor's auction featuring him and Tess. Helene had picked up a few copies for his parents, but he hadn't gotten around to reading the piece. Between issues on the ranch and everything that had been going on with Tess, the article hadn't seemed important.

"And that prompted you to come to Royal because...?"

Sabrina stood, walking over to the fireplace, her back to him for a moment. She turned to face him again.

"It made me think about you. About us. I know we didn't always get along, but when we did, things were really great between us. I miss that." She tucked her blond hair behind her ears as she stepped closer. "I miss you. And I wondered if maybe you missed me, too."

Ryan sighed heavily. Today obviously wasn't his day. The woman he wanted insisted they should just be friends, and the woman he didn't want had traveled halfway across the country hoping to pick up where they'd left off.

He couldn't catch a break.

Ryan leaned forward, both feet firmly on the floor. "Sabrina, we've been through all this. You and I, we're just too different."

"You know what they say." She forced a smile after her initial frown in response to his rejection. "Opposites attract."

"True." He had been intrigued by their differences and because she'd been such a challenge. It had made the chase more exciting. "But in our case, it wasn't enough to maintain a relationship that made either of us happy. In fact, in the end, we were both miserable. Why would you want to go back to that?"

"I'm a different person now. More mature." She joined him on the sofa. "It seems you are, too. The time we've spent away from each other has made me realize what we threw away."

"Sabrina, you're a beautiful woman and there are many things about you that I admire." Ryan sighed. "But you just can't force a square peg into a round hole. This ranch is my life. Always has been, always will be. That hasn't changed. And I doubt that you've suddenly acquired a taste for country living."

"They do build ranches outside of Texas, you know." She flashed her million-dollar smile. "Like in Upstate New York."

"This ranch has been in my family for generations. I have no interest in leaving it behind and starting over in Upstate New York." He inhaled deeply, released his breath slowly, then turned to face her. "And I'm certainly not looking to get involved."

"With me, you mean." Sabrina pushed to her feet and crossed her arms, the phony smile gone. She peered up at him angrily. "You sure seemed eager to 'get involved' with your precious Tess. You went all out for her."

"It was a charity thing. Something we did on behalf of the Texas Cattleman's Club."

"And I suppose you two are still *just* friends?" The question was accusatory, but she didn't pause long enough for him to respond either way.

"Suddenly you're a romantic who rents her fantasy car, knows exactly which flowers she likes, and which wine she drinks?" She laughed bitterly. "I always suspected you two were an item. She's the real reason our relationship died. Not because we're so different or that we want different things."

"Wait. What do you mean Tess is the reason we broke up?"

Sabrina flopped down on the sofa and sighed, shaking her head. "It became painfully obvious that I was the third wheel in the relationship. That I'd never mean as much to you as she does. I deserve better."

Ryan frowned, thinking of his time with Sabrina. Especially the year they'd lived together in Royal before their planned wedding.

He hadn't considered how his relationship with Tessa might have contributed to Sabrina's feelings of isolation. At the time, he'd thought her jealousy of Tess was unwarranted. There certainly hadn't been anything going on between him and Tess back then. Still, in retrospect, he realized the validity of her feelings.

He sat beside Sabrina again. "Maybe I did allow my relationship with Tess to overshadow ours in some ways. For that, I'm sorry. But regardless of the reason for our breakup, the bottom line is, we're just not right for each other. In my book, finding that out before we got married is a good thing."

"What if I don't believe it. What if I believe…" She inhaled deeply, her stormy blue eyes rimmed with tears. "What if I think it was the biggest mistake I ever made, walking away from us?"

"We never could have made each other happy, Brie." He placed his hand over hers and squeezed it. "You would've been miserable living in Royal, even if we had been a perfect match. And God knows I'd be miserable anywhere else. Because this is where my family and friends are. Where my future lies."

"Your future with Tessa?" She pulled her hand from beneath his and used the back of her wrist to wipe away tears.

"My future with Tessa is the same now as it was back then." Regardless of what he wanted. "We're friends."

Sabrina's bitter laugh had turned caustic. She stalked across the floor again. "The sad thing is, I think you two actually believe that."

"What do you mean?"

"You've been in love with each other for as long as I've known you. From what I can tell, probably since the day you two met in diapers. What I don't understand is why, for the love of God, you two don't just admit it. If not to everyone else, at least to yourselves. Then maybe you'd stop hurting those of us insane enough to think we could ever be enough for either of you."

Ryan sat back against the sofa and dragged a hand across his forehead. He'd tried to curtail his feelings for Tess because of his promise to Tripp and because he hadn't wanted to ruin their friendship. But what lay at the root of his denial was his fear that he couldn't be the man Tess deserved. A man as strong as he was loving and unafraid to show his affection for the people he loved.

A man like her father.

In his family, affection was closely aligned with weakness and neediness. In hers, it was just the opposite. With their opposing philosophies on the matter, it was amazing that their parents had managed to become such good friends.

He'd been afraid that he could never measure up to her father and be the man she deserved. But what he hadn't realized was the time he'd spent with Tessa and her family had taught him little by little how to let go of his family's hang-ups and love a woman like Tess.

Sabrina was right. He *was* in love with Tess. Always had been. And he loved her as much more than just a friend. Tessa Noble was the one woman he couldn't imagine not having in his life. And now, he truly understood the depth of his feelings. He needed her to be his friend, his lover, his confidante. He wanted to make love to her every night and wake up to her gorgeous face every morning.

He'd asked Tess to give their relationship a chance, but he hadn't been honest with her or himself about *why* he wanted a relationship with her.

He loved and needed her. Without her in his life, he felt incomplete.

"It wasn't intentional, but I was unfair to you, Sabrina. Our relationship was doomed from the start, because I do love Tess that way. I'm sorry you've come all this way for nothing, but I need to thank you, too. For helping me to realize what I guess I've known on some level all along. That I love Tess, and I want to be with her."

"As long as one of us is happy, right?" Her bangs fluttered when she blew out an exasperated breath.

Ryan stood, offering her an apologetic smile. "C'mon, it's getting late. I'll walk you to your car."

Ryan gave Sabrina a final hug, grateful to her. He'd ask Tess again to give them a chance.

This time, he wouldn't screw it up.

Nineteen

Tessa had been going crazy, pacing in that big old house all alone. She hadn't been able to stop thinking about Ryan. Not just what had happened in the stables, but she'd replayed everything he'd said to her.

She hadn't been fair to him, and she needed to apologize for her part in this whole mess. But first, she thought it best to let him cool off.

Tessa got into her truck and drove into town to have breakfast at the Royal Diner. It was a popular spot in town, so at least she wouldn't be alone.

She ordered coffee and a short stack of pancakes, intending to eat at the counter of the retro diner owned by Sheriff Battle's wife, Amanda. The quaint establishment was frozen in the 1950s with its red, faux-leather booths and black-and-white checkerboard flooring. But Amanda made sure that every surface in the space was gleaming.

"Tessa?"

She turned on her stool toward the booth where someone had called her name.

It was the makeup artist from PURE. Milan Valez.

"Milan. Hey, it's good to see you. How are you this morning?"

"Great. I always pass by this place. Today, I thought I'd stop in and give it a try." Milan's dark eyes shone, and her pecan brown skin was flawless at barely eight in the morning. "I just ordered breakfast. Why don't you join me?"

Tessa let the waitress know she'd be moving, then she slid across from Milan in the corner booth where the woman sat, sipping a glass of orange juice.

When the waitress brought Milan's plate, she indicated that she'd be paying for Tess's meal, too.

"That's kind of you, really, but you're the one who is new in town. I should be treating you," Tess objected.

"I insist." Milan waved a hand. "It's the least I can do after you've brought me so much business. I'm booked up for weeks, thanks to you and that article on the frenzy you caused at the charity auction. Good for you." Milan pointed a finger at her. "I told you that you were a beautiful woman."

"I'm glad everything worked out for at least one of us." Tess muttered the words under her breath, but they were loud enough for the other woman to hear.

"Speaking of which, how is it that you ended up going on this ultra-romantic weekend with your best friend?" Milan tilted her head and assessed Tessa. "And if you two are really 'just friends'—" she used air quotes "—why is it that you look like you are nursing a broken heart?"

Tessa's cheeks burned, and she stammered a bit before taking a long sip of her coffee.

"Don't worry, hon. I don't know enough folks in town to be part of the gossip chain." Milan smiled warmly. "But I've been doing this long enough to recognize a woman having some serious man troubles."

Tessa didn't bother denying it. She took another gulp of her coffee and set her cup on the table. She shook her head and sighed. "I really screwed up."

"By thinking you and your best friend could go on a romantic weekend and still remain just friends?" Milan asked before taking another sip of her orange juice.

"How did you—"

"I told you, been doing this a long time. Makeup artists are like bartenders or hairdressers. Folks sit there in that chair and use it as a confessional." Milan set her glass on the table and smiled. "Besides, I saw those pictures in the paper. That giddy look on your face? That's the look of a woman in love, if ever I've seen it."

"That obvious, huh?"

"Word around town is there's a pool on when you two finally get a clue." Milan laughed.

Tessa buried her face in her hands and moaned. "It's all my fault. He was being a perfect gentleman. I kissed him and then things kind of took off from there."

"And how do you feel about the shift in your relationship with…?"

"Ryan," Tess supplied. She thanked the waitress for her pancakes, poured a generous amount of maple syrup on the stack and cut into them. "I'm not quite sure how to feel about it."

"I'm pretty sure you are." Milan's voice was firm, but kind. "But whatever you're feeling right now, it scares the hell out of you. That's not necessarily a bad thing."

Milan was two for two.

"It's just that we've been best friends for so long. Now everything has changed, and yeah, it is scary. Part of me wants to explore what this could be. Another part of me is terrified of what will happen if everything falls apart. Besides, I'm worried that…" Tessa let the words die on her lips, taking a bite of her pancakes.

"You're worried that…what?" One of Milan's perfectly arched brows lifted.

"That he'll get bored with a Plain Jane like me. That eventually he'll want someone prettier or more glamorous than I could ever be." She shrugged.

"First, glammed up or not, you're nobody's Plain Jane," Milan said pointedly, then offered Tess a warm smile. "Second, that look of love that I saw…it wasn't just in your eyes. It was there in his, too."

Tessa paused momentarily, contemplating Milan's observation. She was a makeup artist, not a mind reader, for goodness' sake. So it was best not to put too much stock in the woman's words. Still, it made her hopeful. Besides, there was so much more to the friendship she and Rye had built over the years.

They'd supported one another. Confided in

each other. Been there for each other through the best and worst of times. She recalled Ryan's words when he'd stormed out of the stables the previous night.

They *were* good together. Compatible in all the ways that mattered. And she couldn't imagine her life without him.

"Only you can determine whether it's worth the risk to lean into your feelings for your friend, or if you're better off running as fast as you can in the opposite direction." Milan's words broke into her thoughts. The woman took a bite of her scrambled eggs. "What's your gut telling you?"

"To go for the safest option. But that's always been my approach to my love life, which is why I haven't had much of one." Tessa chewed another bite of her pancakes. "In a perfect world, sure I'd take a chance. See where this relationship might lead. But—"

"There's no such thing as a perfect world, darlin'." A smile lit Milan's eyes. "As my mama always said, nothing ventured, nothing gained. You can either allow fear to prevent you from going for what you really want, or you can grow a set of lady *cojones*, throw caution to the wind, and confess your feelings to your friend. You might discover that he feels the same way about you. Maybe he's afraid of risking his heart, too."

Milan pointed her fork at Tessa. "The question you have to ask yourself is—is what you two could have together worth risking any embarrassment or hurt feelings?"

"Yes." The word burst from her lips without a second of thought. Still, its implication left her stunned, her hands shaking.

A wide smile lit the other woman's face. "Then why are you still sitting here with me? Girl, you need to go and get your man, before someone else does. Someone who isn't afraid."

Tess grabbed two pieces of bacon and climbed to her feet, adrenaline pumping through her veins. "I'm sorry, Milan. Rain check?"

"You know where to find me." She nodded toward the door. "Now go, before you lose your nerve."

Tessa gave the woman an awkward hug, then

she hurried out of the diner, determined to tell
Ryan the truth.

She was in love with him.

Ryan was evidently even angrier with Tessa
than she'd thought. She'd called him repeatedly
with no answer. She'd even gone over to the Bateman Ranch, but Helene said he'd left first thing
in the morning and she didn't expect him until
evening. Then she mentioned that his ex, Sabrina,
had been at the house the day before.

Tess's heart sank. Had her rejection driven
Ryan back into the arms of his ex?

She asked Helene to give her a call the second
Ryan's truck pulled into the driveway, and she
begged her not to let Ryan know.

The woman smiled and promised she would,
giving Tess a huge hug before she left.

Tessa tried to go about her day as normally as
possible. She started by calling Bo and Clem and
apologizing for any misunderstanding. Both men
were disappointed, but gracious about it.

When Tripp arrived back home from the airport, he brought her up to speed on the potential client. He'd landed the account. She hugged her brother and congratulated him, standing with him when he video conferenced their parents and told them the good news.

Tripp wanted to celebrate, but she wasn't in the mood to go out, and he couldn't get a hold of Ryan, either. So he called up Lana, since it was her day off.

Tessa had done every ranch chore she could think of to keep her mind preoccupied, until finally Roy Jensen ran her off, tired of her being underfoot.

When Roy and the other stragglers had gone, she was left with nothing but her thoughts about what she'd say to Ryan once she saw him.

Finally, when she'd stepped out of the shower, Helene called, whispering into the phone that Ryan had just pulled into the drive of the Bateman Ranch.

Tessa hung up the phone, dug out her makeup bag and got ready for the scariest moment of her life.

* * *

Ryan hopped out of the shower, threw on a clean shirt and a pair of jeans. He picked up the gray box and stuck it in his pocket, not caring that his hair was still wet. He needed to see Tess.

He hurried downstairs. The entire first floor of the ranch smelled like the brisket Helene had been slow-cooking all day. But as tempted as he was by Helene's heavenly cooking, his stomach wasn't his priority. It would have to wait a bit longer.

"I was beginning to think you'd dozed off up there. And this brisket smells so good. It took every ounce of my willpower not to nab a piece." Tessa stood in the kitchen wearing a burgundy, cowl-neck sweater dress that hit her mid-thigh. "I mean, it would be pretty rude to start eating your dinner before you've had any."

"Tessa." He'd been desperate to see her, but now that she was here, standing in front of him, his pulse raced and his heart hammered against his ribs. "What are you doing here?"

She frowned, wringing her hands before forcing a smile. "I really needed to talk to you. Helene let me in before she left. Please don't be mad at her."

"No, of course I'm not mad at Helene."

"But you are still angry with me?" She stepped closer, peering up at him intensely.

"I'm not angry with you, Tess. I…" He sighed, running a hand through his wet hair.

He'd planned a perfect evening for them. Had gone over the words he wanted to say again and again. But seeing her now, none of that mattered. "But I do need to talk to you. And, despite the grand plans that I'd made, I just need to get this out."

"What is it, Rye?" Tessa worried her lower lip with her teeth. "What is it you need to tell me?" When he didn't answer right away, she added, "I know Sabrina was here yesterday. Did you two… are you back together?"

"Sabrina and me? God, no. What happened with us was for the best. She may not see it now, but one day she will."

Tessa heaved a sigh of relief. "Okay, so what do you need to tell me?"

Ryan reached for her hand and led her to the sofa in the family room just off the kitchen. Seated beside her, he turned his body toward hers and swallowed the huge lump in his throat.

"Tess, you've been my best friend since we were both knee-high to a grasshopper. The best moments of my life always involve you. You're always there with that big, bright smile and those warm, brown eyes, making me believe I can do anything. That I deserve everything. And I'm grateful that you've been my best friend all these years."

Tess cradled his cheek with her free hand. The corners of her eyes were wet with tears. She nodded. "Me, too. You've always been there for me, Ryan. I guess we've both been pretty lucky, huh?"

"We have been. But I've also been pretty foolish. Selfish even. Because I wanted you all to myself. Was jealous of any man who dared infringe on your time, or God forbid, command your attention. But I was afraid to step up and be the man you deserved."

"*Was* afraid?'" Now the tears flowed down her face more rapidly. She wiped them away with the hand that had cradled his face a moment ago. "As in past tense?"

"*Am* terrified would be more accurate." He forced a smile as he gently wiped the tears from her cheek with his thumb. "But just brave enough to tell you that I love you, Tessa Noble, and not just as a friend. I love you with all my heart. You're everything to me, and I couldn't imagine my life without you."

"I love you, too, Rye." Tessa beamed. "I mean, I'm in love with you. I have been for so long, I'm not really even sure when it shifted from you being my best friend to you being the guy I was head over heels in love with."

"Tess." He kissed her, then pulled her into his arms. "You have no idea how happy I am right now."

Relief flooded his chest and his heart felt full, as if it might burst. He loved this woman, who also happened to be his best friend. He loved her more than anything in the world. And he wanted to be with her.

Always.

For the first time in his life, the thought of spending the rest of his days with the same woman didn't give him a moment's pause. Because Tessa Noble had laid claim to his heart long ago. She was the one woman whose absence from his life would make him feel incomplete. Like a man functioning with only half of his heart.

"Tessa, would you…" He froze for a moment. His tongue sticking to the roof of his mouth. Not because he was afraid. Nor was he having second thoughts. There were a few things he needed to do first.

"What is it, Ryan?" She looked up at him, her warm, brown eyes full of love and light. The same eyes he'd been enamored with for as long as he could remember.

"I'd planned to take you out to dinner. Maybe catch a movie. But since Helene has already made such an amazing meal…"

"It'd be a shame to waste it." A wicked smile lit her beautiful face. "So why don't we eat dinner here, and then afterward…" She kissed him, her delicate hands framing his face. "Let's just say that dinner isn't the only thing I'm hungry for."

"That makes two of us." He pulled her into the kitchen and made them plates of Helene's delicious meal before they ended up naked and starving.

After their quick meal, Ryan swept Tessa into his arms and kissed her. Then he took her up to his bedroom where he made love to his best friend.

This time there was no uncertainty. No hesitation. No regrets. His heart and his body belonged to Tessa Noble. Now and always.

Ryan woke at nearly two in the morning and patted the space beside him. The space where Tess had lain, her bottom cuddled against his length. Her spot was still warm.

He raised up on his elbows and looked around.

She was in the corner of the room, wiggling back into her dress.

"Hey, beautiful." He scrubbed the sleep from his eye. "Where are you going?"

"Sorry, I didn't mean to wake you." She turned a lamp on beside the chair.

"You're leaving?" He sat up fully, drawing his knees up and resting his arms on them when she nodded in response. "Why?"

"Because until we talk to our families about this, I thought it best we be discreet."

"But it's not like you haven't spent the night here before," he groused, already missing the warmth of her soft body cuddled against his. It was something he'd missed every night since their return from Dallas.

"I know, but things are different now. I'm not just sleeping in the guest room." She gave him a knowing look.

"You've slept in here before, too."

"When we fell asleep binge-watching all the Marvel movies. And we both fell asleep fully dressed." She slipped on one of her boots and zipped it. "Not when I can't stop smiling because we had the most amazing night together. Tripp would see through that in two seconds."

He was as elated by her statement as he was disappointed by her leaving. What she was saying made sense. Of course, it did. But he wanted her in his bed, in his life. Full stop.

Tessa deserved better than the two of them sneaking around. Besides, with that came the implication that the two of them were doing something wrong. They weren't. And he honestly couldn't wait to tell everyone in town just how much he loved Tessa Noble.

"I'll miss you, too, babe." She sat on the edge of the bed beside him and planted a soft kiss on his lips.

Perhaps she'd only intended for the kiss to placate him. But he'd slipped his hands beneath her skirt and glided them up to the scrap of fabric covering her sex.

She murmured her objection, but Ryan had swallowed it with his hungry kiss. Lips searching and tongues clashing. His needy groans countered her small whimpers of pleasure.

"Rye… I really need to go." Tess pulled away momentarily.

He resumed their kiss as he led her hand to his growing length.

"Guess it would be a shame to waste something that impressive." A wicked smile flashed across Tess's beautiful face. She encircled his warm flesh in her soft hand as she glided it up and down his straining shaft. "Maybe I could stay a little longer. Just let me turn off the light."

"No," he whispered against the soft, sweet lips he found irresistible. "Leave it on. I want to see you. All of you."

He pulled the dress over her head and tossed it aside. Then he showed Tess just how much he appreciated her staying a little while longer.

Twenty

Ryan waved Tripp to the booth he'd secured at the back of the Daily Grind.

Tripp was an uncomplicated guy who always ordered the same thing. At the Royal Diner, a stack of pancakes, two eggs over easy, crispy bacon and black coffee. Here at the Daily Grind, a bear claw that rivaled the size of one's head and a cup of black coffee, two sugars.

Ryan had placed their order as soon as he'd arrived, wanting to get right down to their conversation.

His friend slid into the booth and looked at the

plate on the table and his cup of coffee. "You already ordered for me?"

"Don't worry. It's still hot. I picked up our order two minutes ago."

Tripp sipped his coffee. "Why do I have the feeling that I'm about to get some really bad news?"

"Depends on your point of view, I guess." Ryan shoved the still warm cinnamon bun aside, his hands pressed to the table.

"It must be really bad. Did something happen to our parents on the cruise?"

"It's nothing like that." Ryan swallowed hard, tapping the table lightly. He looked up squarely at his friend. "I just… I need to tell you that I broke my promise to you…about Tess." Ryan sat back in the booth. "Tripp, I love her. I think I always have."

"I see." Tripp's gaze hardened. "Since you're coming to me with this, it's probably safe to assume you're already sleeping with my little sister."

Ryan didn't respond either way. He owed Tripp

this, but the details of their relationship, that was between him and Tess. They didn't owe anyone else an explanation.

"Of course." Tripp nodded, his fists clenched on the table in front of him. "That damn auction. The gift that keeps on giving."

Ryan half expected his friend to try to slug him, as he had when they were teenagers and the kids at school had started a rumor that Ryan was Tess's boyfriend. It was the last time the two of them had an honest-to-goodness fight.

That was when Tripp had made him promise he'd never lay a hand on Tess.

"Look, Tripp, I know you didn't think I was good enough for your sister. Deep down, I think I believed that, too. But more than anything I was afraid to ruin my friendship with her or you. You and Tess…you're more than just friends to me. You're family."

"If you were so worried about wrecking our friendships, what's changed? Why are you suddenly willing to risk it?" Tripp folded his arms as he leaned on the table.

"I've changed. Or at least, my perspective has. I can't imagine watching your sister live a life with someone else. Marrying some other guy and raising their children. Wishing they were ours." Ryan shook his head. "That's a regret I can't take to my grave. And if it turns out I'm wrong, I honestly believe my friendship with you and Tess is strong enough to recover. But the thing is... I don't think I am wrong about us. I love her, Tripp, and I'm gonna ask her to marry me. But I wanted to come to you first and explain why I could no longer keep my promise."

"You're planning to propose? Already? God, what the hell happened with you guys in Dallas?" Tripp shut his eyes and shook his head. "Never mind. On second thought, don't *ever* tell me what happened in Dallas."

"Now that's a promise I'm pretty sure I can keep." Ryan chuckled.

"I guess it could be worse. She could be marrying some dude I hate instead of one of my best friends."

It was as close to a blessing as he was likely to get from Tripp. He'd gladly take it.

"Thanks, man. That means a lot. I promise, I won't let you or Tess down."

"You'd better not." Tripp picked up his bear claw and took a huge bite.

It was another promise he had every intention of keeping.

Ryan, Tessa, Tripp and both sets of their parents, had dinner at the Glass House restaurant at the exclusive five-star Bellamy resort to celebrate their parents' return and Tripp landing the Noble Spur's biggest customer account to date.

The restaurant was decked out in festive holiday decor. Two beautiful Douglas firs. Twinkling lights everywhere. Red velvet bows and poinsettias. Then there were gifts wrapped in shiny red, green, gold and silver foil wrapping paper.

Tessa couldn't be happier. She was surrounded by the people who meant the most to her. And both her parents and Ryan's had been thrilled that she and Ryan had finally acknowledged what both their mothers claimed to have known all along. That she and Ryan were hopelessly in love.

Ryan had surprised her with an early Christmas gift—the Maybach saddle she'd mused about on their drive to Dallas.

Even Tripp was impressed.

The food at the Glass House was amazing, as always. And a live act, consisting of a vocalist and an acoustic guitar player, set the mood by serenading the patrons with soft ballads.

When they started to play Christina Perri's "A Thousand Years," Ryan asked her to dance. Next, the duo performed Train's song, "Marry Me."

"I love that song. It's so perfect." Tessa swayed happily to the music as the vocalist sang the romantic lyrics.

"It is." He grinned. "And so are you. I'm so lucky that the woman I love is also my best friend. You, Tess, are the best Christmas gift I could ever hope for."

"That's so sweet of you to say, babe." Her cheeks flushed and her eyes shone with tears. She smiled. "Who says you're not romantic?"

"You make me want to be. Because you deserve it all. Romance, passion, friendship. A home of our own, marriage, kids. You deserve all of that and more. And I want to be the man who gives that to you."

Tessa blinked back tears. "Ryan, it sounds a lot like you're asking me to marry you."

"Guess that means I ain't doing it quite right." Ryan winked and pulled a gray velvet box from his pocket. He opened it and Tessa gasped, covering her mouth with both hands as he got down on one knee and took her left hand in his.

"Tessa Marie Noble, you're my best friend, my lover, my confidante. You've always been there for me, Tess. And I always want to be there for you, making an incredible life together right here in the town we both love. Would you please do me the great honor of being my wife?"

"Yes." Tessa nodded, tears rolling down her cheeks. "Nothing would make me happier than marrying my best friend."

Ryan slipped on the ring and kissed her hand. He'd known the moment he'd seen the ring that it was the one for Tess. As unique and beautiful as the woman he loved. A chocolate diamond solitaire set in a strawberry gold band of intertwined ribbons sprinkled with vanilla and chocolate diamonds.

Tessa extended her hand and studied the ring, a wide grin spreading across her gorgeous face. "It's my Neapolitan engagement ring!"

"Anything for you, babe." Ryan took her in his arms and kissed her with their families and fellow diners cheering them on.

But for a few moments, everyone else disappeared, and there was only Tessa Noble. The woman who meant everything to him, and always would.

* * * * *

LET'S TALK

Romance

For exclusive extracts, competitions and special offers, find us online:

- facebook.com/millsandboon
- @millsandboonuk
- @millsandboon

Or get in touch on 0844 844 1351*

For all the latest titles coming soon, visit millsandboon.co.uk/nextmonth

Want even more
ROMANCE?

Join our bookclub today!

Visit millsandbook.co.uk/Bookclub and save on brand new books.

MILLS & BOON